The Tea Shop

De-ann Black

Toffee Apple Publishing

Other books in the Sewing, Knitting & Baking book series are:

Book 1 - The Tea Shop.
Book 2 - The Sewing Bee & Afternoon Tea.
Book 3 - The Christmas Knitting Bee.
Book 4 – Champagne Chic Lemonade Money.
Book 5 – The Vintage Sewing & Knitting Bee.

Text copyright © 2018 by De-ann Black
Cover Design & Illustration © 2018 by De-ann Black

All rights reserved.
No part of this book may be used or reproduced in any manner whatsoever without the written consent of the publisher.

This is a work of fiction. Names, characters, places, and incidents are either products of the author's imagination or are used fictitiously. Any resemblance to actual persons, living or dead, businesses, companies, events, or locales is entirely coincidental.

First published 2014

Published by Toffee Apple Publishing 2018

The Tea Shop

ISBN: 9781976981302

Toffee Apple Publishing

Also by De-ann Black (Romance, Action/Thrillers & Children's books). See her Amazon Author page or website for further details about her books, screenplays, illustrations, art and fabric designs.
www.De-annBlack.com

Romance:

The Sewing Shop
Heather Park
The Tea Shop by the Sea
The Bookshop by the Seaside
The Sewing Bee
The Quilting Bee
Snow Bells Wedding
Snow Bells Christmas
Summer Sewing Bee
The Chocolatier's Cottage
Christmas Cake Chateau
The Beemaster's Cottage
The Sewing Bee By The Sea
The Flower Hunter's Cottage
The Christmas Knitting Bee
The Sewing Bee & Afternoon Tea
The Vintage Sewing & Knitting Bee
Shed In The City
The Bakery By The Seaside
Champagne Chic Lemonade Money
The Christmas Chocolatier
The Christmas Tea Shop & Bakery
The Vintage Tea Dress Shop In Summer
Oops! I'm The Paparazzi
The Bitch-Proof Suit

Action/Thrillers:

Love Him Forever.
Someone Worse.
Electric Shadows.
The Strife Of Riley.
Shadows Of Murder.

Children's books:

Faeriefied.
Secondhand Spooks.
Poison-Wynd.
Wormhole Wynd.
Science Fashion.
School For Aliens.

Colouring books:

Summer Garden. Spring Garden. Autumn Garden. Sea Dream. Festive Christmas. Christmas Garden. Flower Bee. Wild Garden. Faerie Garden Spring. Flower Hunter. Stargazer Space. Bee Garden.

Embroidery books:

Floral Nature Embroidery Designs
Scottish Garden Embroidery Designs

Contents

1 - The Pop–Up Girl	1
2 - The Tea Shop & Vintage Cakes	11
3 - Ice Cream Cake	21
4 - Shortbread & Stealth	28
5 - Champagne Afternoon Tea Party	39
6 - Fondant Tea Roses & Birthday Cake	49
7 - Tea by the Sea	57
8 - Ice cream & Scandalous Behaviour	67
9 - The Tea Dance	76
10 - Cakes, Scones & Romance	86
About De-ann Black	94

Chapter One

The Pop-Up Girl

Brodan McBride was as rich and desirable as the cakes he made. A master pastry chef, he was no doubt a challenge to work with, but I was determined to focus on the job and resist his dark, brooding looks.

I knew the first time I saw him that he would be an indulgence as tempting as his baking and confections. I tried to hide the effect he had on me especially as he had me in his sights.

'So you're the pop–up girl?' His voice questioned what he already knew. He was the one who had emailed me seeking shop premises for late spring and summer.

'Yes,' I said, 'that's sort of my nickname.'

The exquisite hazel eyes flickered with amusement. 'It suits you.'

I wasn't sure he meant it as a compliment.

We'd agreed to meet in a cafe bar in a seaside town on the West Coast of Scotland. Brodan was based in Glasgow. Neither of us had an office in the town, so this was neutral territory for our initial chat about his business. I was on time but he was already there.

At thirty–two, he was four years older than me. Although my heels added to my five–four height, he towered above me. All six–foot plus of his athletic physique cast a sexy shadow over my slender frame.

I fought the urge to fuss with my blonde hair. I wore it down, smooth, settled around the shoulders of my deep red business suit. I always felt confident when I wore it. It flattered my slim figure, giving me womanly curves that nature had failed to supply. Brodan's handsome features didn't register his thoughts and it was the first time my confidence wasn't quite up to the mark.

We shook hands. His hand was strong and enveloped mine. His clothes were classic. A three–piece dark suit, white shirt and tie. Money. Class. He owned a mansion in Glasgow and his bakery business was based there.

I stood my ground in front of his broad–shouldered build that overshadowed me in both power and wealth. I did okay for money these days, but I hadn't forgotten the lean times when I could barely afford to keep the rent payments up on my flat. It would take time before I felt financially secure even though I was making a decent living from my business.

Sexy eyes looked down at me, appraising me with a depth that made me blush. His jaw had a hint of dark stubble that I knew would feel quite sexy against my cheeks if I kissed him. Lips like his were made for hot nights and smouldering summer kisses...

I blinked out of my thoughts. It had been a long day and I couldn't entirely trust myself not to say what I was thinking or act on impulse, something that had caused nothing but mayhem in the past. Despite being what most people call a sensible young woman, I have my moments, usually when sensual men are involved.

He secured a table for us in a quiet alcove. I sat down opposite him and put a folder filled with a list of shop properties on the table.

My experience in marketing and PR had helped me create a business that found temporary premises for various types of shops. Mainly it was fashion businesses seeking a shop to launch a new collection or shop space within a well–established department store. The recession had created demand for the hire of empty shop premises on a temporary basis. Most wanted to hire a shop for a month, though shorter or longer leases were available.

Brodan explained in his email that he wanted me to find him suitable premises in one of the seaside towns where he could set up a traditional tea shop selling cakes, ice cream and afternoon tea during the spring and summer. His parents lived in a large mansion in the area and were on an extended holiday abroad in America. He'd agreed to look after their house while they were away. After that, he'd leave and go back to Glasgow. He'd also decided to try to gain further interest in his bakery and confectionary products in the coastal town while living there. And I was the pop–up girl, as I'd become known, that he had chosen to work with.

We ordered tea and I opened the folder to begin our chat.

'You were recommended to me by friends,' he said. 'They spoke highly of your reputation for finding suitable premises for hire.'

I sipped my tea. 'I handle vacant premises, and other businesses who are willing to provide guest space for the likes of yourself.'

'I'm looking for a shop that's on the coast. I gave you a list of the areas I'm interested in.'

'Unfortunately, most of the vacant premises in those keys areas have been snapped up. Spring and summer are popular times for pop–up ventures.'

He looked at the folder. 'What do you have left available?'

I already knew what would suit him, having whittled it down to two shops that would provide the type of set–up he'd need. 'This shop is small but it's available until the end of July.' I checked my calendar. 'The lease starts on the first week in May, so that would give you two weeks to get it ready.'

'I'm looking to open my pop–up tea shop immediately,' he reminded me. 'I'm happy to pay for extra rental time so that I can start getting it up and running. And as I'll be including champagne afternoon teas I need the premises to be licensed for serving alcohol.'

'Well, this is for hire. As I say, it's a small shop but it has the advantage of an excellent kitchen facility. It used to be a cafe and bar and the display counter and other fittings are included in the lease.'

I showed him photographs of the premises. He nodded as he studied them.

'I've also got this shop. It was originally a tearoom and then it was a bar/restaurant but they retained the tearoom fixtures and design. The styling is classic. Lots of dark wood with cream walls and lovely vintage lamps, shades, curtains, display dressers, a counter and other accessories. Everything, as per the agreement, has been cleaned and maintained. The kitchen is adequate I think, but in need of modernising, though you'll know what suits you better than me.'

I opened the folder and he studied the photographs and details of the vacant tearoom.

'I like the look of the tearoom,' he said. 'I can work with any kitchen, within reason of course.'

Both premises were situated in the busy coastal town where we were meeting, and if I'd been him, I'd have chosen the tearoom. I loved the vintage theme of it, especially the front window that I envisaged would look wonderful done up like something from a bygone era.

'I can take you to have a look at the premises if you'd like,' I offered. 'It's further along the main street.'

We left the cafe bar, and with him towering above me, we navigated through the busy Saturday shoppers and drizzling rain. April showers had been frequent but the forecast was for a lovely mild May. I put up my umbrella. My car was parked at the far side of the street but the tearoom was nearby so it was easier to walk there. Brodan didn't seem to notice the rain and had a determined look on his face, taking in the type of people who were shopping in the area.

All types of people were hurrying along doing their shopping. The lights from the shops glittered across the streets, creating sparkles through the rainy atmosphere.

I led him over to the tearoom. Even with no lights on, the old–fashioned exterior looked inviting. Well, I thought it did. It was difficult to tell what he thought. I'd checked him out on the internet before our meeting. According to what I'd seen, and from his website, he was born in Scotland but had spent a considerable amount of time living, working, travelling and training to become a master baker in various cities, including London and New York. His sexy Scottish accent had a hint of having been abroad. The sound of his voice sent pleasing sensations through me, though I tried not to think of him like that. This was business. Once I'd set him up in his tea shop, I'd arrange for the lease payments to be made from him to the rental owner, and then add my fee to the transaction.

The owners of the tearoom premises were people I'd worked with a few times, and they were happy to entrust the keys to me to let clients have a look around.

We stepped inside and I flicked the lights on. The shop had a warmth to it even though the rainy April day was rather chilly. The floral rose curtains had been cleaned and hung back up and I loved the antique dark wood tables and chairs. Somewhere in the past, the tearoom had been brimming with pots of tea and chatter. Photographs I'd seen when I first viewed the premises fascinated me. Cake stands were topped with scones and served with jam and clotted cream for afternoon tea along with raspberry and buttercream sponge, Ayrshire shortbread, petticoat tails, butterfly cakes, marmalade slices, tea loaf, and coffee and walnut cake. Dainty cucumber sandwiches sat enticingly beside smoked salmon sandwiches made from brown bread with the crusts cut off. Preserves, pickles and wholegrain mustard were presented in little jars or dishes with silver serving spoons. I noticed that the teapots were silver rather than ceramic, though I loved both. The setting cheered me up just looking at it and I hoped that someone...perhaps a man like Brodan McBride, would bring it back to life again. The thought of enjoying tea and baking served as it was in the past made me smile thinking about it.

The tall figure of Brodan went through to the kitchen. 'This would be ideal. I like the older kitchen. The catering ovens look well–maintained and the layout is efficient.'

He came out of the kitchen and looked around. 'The location is perfect. Lots of shoppers going past the front window. And a stone's throw from the sea.'

A staircase led to the storeroom upstairs.

'There's also the benefit of having the room upstairs,' I said. 'From photographs I've seen of the original tearoom it was used to serve teas. Four small tables were set upstairs but the previous clients used it for storage.'

He couldn't wait to see upstairs and I followed him up the little wooden staircase. He'd already found the dumbwaiter for conveying food from one floor to the other tucked beside a serving hatch by the time my heels had navigated the stairs.

'I noticed that the kitchen has a storeroom and a pantry cupboard,' he said. 'These would be adequate for storage and would allow me to use this floor as part of the tea shop.'

I could hear the enthusiasm in his voice.

'You'd need to add new curtains to the windows. The old curtains were taken down and never replaced.'

He peered out one of the windows at the busy streets and the seashore. 'Perfect,' he murmured, almost to himself. 'This would work. I could make this work.'

I didn't doubt it. From what I'd seen featured on his website, Brodan was capable of creating a tea shop here that would be a match for the one he had in Glasgow. He'd explained that he had a manager and staff running the one in Glasgow, allowing him to venture down the coast and open the pop–up tea shop. I sensed that he was a man who enjoyed a challenge. I couldn't help but admire him — in more ways than one.

We went back downstairs.

'Would you like to see the other premises?' I said.

'No, I'll take this.'

'I have the lease agreement here if you'd like to have a read over it. It's similar to the one I emailed to you. Mainly it's to secure payment upfront. Insurance is included in the fee. Have a read over it, and —'

'Can I sign it now?'

'Eh, yes, but surely you want to consider it.'

He took out a pen from his inside jacket pocket and set the lease agreement down on the shop counter. 'Where do I sign?'

I stepped close and felt my heart skip a few beats. He was gorgeous. 'Sign there.'

He signed and then wrote a cheque for the full amount and handed it to me.

We agreed that he could move in immediately. As with all the pop–up premises I dealt with, they were already clean and fit for use.

'I don't know how you plan to hire staff,' I said, 'but here is a contact number for a reliable company. They hire out catering and shop staff. I've recommended them to other businesses and everyone's been pleased with their work.'

He accepted the card and put it in his pocket. 'That was very helpful of you...'

'Jayne.'

He seemed embarrassed that he'd forgotten my name, but then again, I was just the pop–up girl to him.

'Thank you, Jayne. You've been very efficient.'

'Let me know if you need anything else. You have my email and mobile number.'

'There is one thing.'

I looked at him.

'Have dinner with me tonight.'

'Me?' *The pop–up girl*? What did rich and sexy Brodan McBride want with me?

'I have a proposition I'd like to put to you. I thought we could discuss it over dinner tonight.'

'A business proposition?'

The hazel eyes flicked across my features. 'Yes. What other kind of proposition were you thinking of?'

Don't tempt me, I thought to myself. A night of passion, running my hands over that taut stomach and leanly muscled chest of his.

And kissing those sensuous lips that had yet to smile at me. I felt a blush burn across my cheeks. 'No other kind,' I lied.

He smiled, and I melted. It was easier to deal with him when he looked mean.

'I see that your address is near here,' he said, reading my contact details.

'Yes, I live above one of the shops.'

'Perhaps you can recommend somewhere nearby where we could have dinner. I haven't been down here a lot recently. My parents usually come to Glasgow to visit me.'

I recommended a couple of restaurants and we agreed on one.

I went back to my flat above the shop and wondered why I felt so excited about having dinner with Brodan. He was just a handsome, rich and sexy single man. Dinner was business. Not a date. He wasn't interested in me. Men like him dated models, beautiful women. I was okay with a bit of makeup. In the past two years since I'd set up my pop–up business, I'd hardly had time to date. My last boyfriend was ages ago.

I was trawling through my wardrobe for something suitable to wear when Brodan phoned.

'I'm sorry, but something's come up. Business. I'll have to cancel our dinner this evening.'

'That's fine,' I said, hiding my disappointment, feeling my excitement fizzle out like a damp squib.

'I'll call soon to reschedule,' he promised.

Two weeks went past and he never did.

The shop lights sparkled in the rain. At around five in the evening shoppers scurried along the wet streets, popping into the boutiques and other shops for warmth and shelter. The town offered a fantastic range of shops, and in the three years I'd lived there, I'd never tired of finding yet another wonderful shop or product within its magnificent niche.

Situated on the beautiful West Coast, the town had a bright and colourful mix of shops and businesses.

I'd been brought up in Glasgow and lived there all my life, but I'd moved from the city to the coast and lived in a flat above one of the shops I hired out when it became available for rent. It was handy for work and I loved the buzz of the area.

It had been a busy week and a particularly busy Thursday. I headed up to the flat and closed my door against the hectic world.

I flopped down on the sofa and kicked my boots off. I was planning a night in, feet up, glass of wine and relaxing in front of the television when an email pinged into my laptop. I kept the laptop open because clients emailed in the evenings as well as during business hours.

The email was from Brodan. An invitation to the opening night of his tea shop. How could I resist? An evening of sampling his delicious cakes, sipping champagne, mingling with people who could be potential clients, and stepping into Brodan McBride's world. Though perhaps the latter wasn't a great idea.

My phone rang. It was him.

'I emailed you.'

Yes, all of about a few minutes ago.

'Some people don't check their emails and I wanted to make sure you got it.'

'Yes, I was about to reply.'

'Great. So you'll be there at the opening?'

'Wouldn't miss it.'

'Excellent. I'll see you tomorrow night.'

After another hectic day, Ceard welcomed me into his hair salon. I shook the rain from my umbrella and put it in the stand near the window.

He kissed me on both cheeks. 'Come on in. You look stressed.' He beckoned one of the salon assistants. 'Tea for Jayne. Milk no sugar. She's sweet enough.' He ushered me towards one of the chairs and sat me down in front of the mirror. His hands had already started lifting up the lacklustre strands of my damp hair with an enthusiasm that never failed to emerge whenever I saw him.

'I need to look irresistible.'

He pretended to check his salon list, running his finger down the items and frowning. 'Ah yes, here we are. We have irresistible and totally irresistible. The latter costs slightly more.'

'I'll splurge.'

We laughed. We'd been friends since school and money rarely exchanged hands. We had lunch and met up regularly to gossip and pour out our woes when a relationship went wrong. He was my dearest male friend, like the brother I'd never had. I'd always wanted to be part of a big, boisterous family. I had no siblings and my parents had lived abroad, in New York, since I was in my late teens. We weren't close, and not just because of the large expanse of sea, but because they wanted a daughter who was totally brilliant and that definitely wasn't me. My parents hated fuss and I seemed to manufacture it wherever I went. Not intentionally. I tried not to cause chaos, but like wisps from a dandelion clock it tended to waft around me.

And I was happy in Scotland and didn't want to move abroad. When it came to Christmas and other party occasions, I shared Ceard's relatives. I'd felt part of his family on many occasions when our schedules allowed. He was usually as busy as me.

Ceard smiled at me in the mirror. 'So, who is the lucky guy?'

'Brodan McBride, a master at creating vintage patisserie. He's a new pop–up client. He's opened a tea shop near here serving traditional tea and classic cakes, ice cream and old–fashioned baking.'

'Oooh, a master? Sounds adventurous. Does his light sabre glow in the dark? Or is tonight the first time you'll have the pleasure of finding out?'

'Out. Of. My. League.'

'No man is out of your league sweetie, believe me. If we hadn't been brought up like brother and sister, I'd have totally swept you off your pretty little feet. Speaking of which...' He glared down at my wet boots.

'I know, I know. I've been traipsing around all day and these boots were made for fashion not the rain.'

'Take them off.'

A woman sitting having her hair done further along glanced at him.

'Her boots, not her clothes, darling.'

'Tell me all about this Brodan McBride chap. What's his story? Is he single? Is he gorgeous? Am I finally going to lose you to yet another broken heart?'

'I'm done with men.'

He pretended to adjust his hearing, tugging at his ear. 'I'm sorry? What was that? I thought I heard you say you were done with men.'

'For now. For spring. For summer. Maybe into the autumn. Done, done, done.'

'I thought you were over Oliver.'

'I am.' This was true. I was. I don't even know what I saw in him. Oliver was a mistake.

'So why the curfew on love?'

'I need a break from heartache. I'm tired of running around after men who muck me about. If only more men were like you.'

'Great at deep conditioning and an absolute colour genius?'

'Exactly.'

We giggled.

'And a gossip magnet,' he added, whispering over my shoulder.

'What's the gossip?'

'Can't tell you here.' He flicked at glance at the glaring women.

'Come with me to the party tonight,' I said. 'The invitation extends to bring a friend.'

He pondered my suggestion.

'There's champagne,' I said. 'And cake and ice cream.'

'I'm in. I guess I'll have to look totally irresistible too.'

'You always look handsome.'

He threw me a wicked smile. 'You're just saying that because it's true.'

Chapter Two

The Tea Shop & Vintage Cakes

By seven, we were both totally irresistible or as much as I could manage. I wore a little vintage dress that I'd bought from a second-hand shop that sold amazing preloved bargain clothes. It sparkled with crystal beads.

Ceard had put a shine rinse through my hair and it was glossy to the max.

Ceard wore a dark suit and an open–neck shirt. His silky brown hair was well-styled and although he wasn't as tall as Brodan, Ceard still made me look small. His most attractive feature was his smile, but when he was mad at me for something I gave top billing to his lovely blue eyes. He didn't get mad at me very often even though I had a tendency to involve him in my chaotic life. Patience was certainly one of his virtues along with the ability to make my blonde hair look like it had enjoyed a summer's worth of sun instead of being soaked by the April rain. Any woman who got Ceard was on to a winner. He'd even advised me on my makeup. 'Wear sparkly silver on the inner corners of your eyes. You look a bit tired. That'll brighten you up.'

We approached the tea shop. It was all aglow. The upstairs windows were lit up and I liked the patterned curtains Brodan had used for them — fairy cake fabric on one window and a lovely ice cream print on the other. Pretty bunting wafted in the mild evening breeze. Outside the entrance stood a vintage blue bicycle with the basket full of flowers — roses, delphiniums and trailing greenery.

The front window was done up with silver cake stands, vintage teapots and traditional baking. Victoria sponges, Battenberg, butterfly cakes with buttercream icing, scones, chocolate fudge cake and ice cream tempted us inside.

The shop had a warm atmosphere with plenty of people enjoying various cakes, chatting and sipping tea.

Ceard whispered to me. 'Did we just enter a time warp? It looks like we stepped back into the 1940s, maybe even earlier. If I'd paid more attention to history in school I could've nailed it closer, but you know what I mean.'

I did. The tea shop with its tables set with white linen and silverware looked like a slice of the past. Everything from the napkins to the tea strainers created an ambiance of earlier days when there was time to enjoy the finer things in life — like Champagne Afternoon Tea, as was advertised on the menus. Ice Cream Teas caught my attention as did the list of patisserie. The words chocolate, cream, strawberries and indulgence popped out at me as I skimmed over the menus. There was a menu for morning tea, afternoon tea and speciality teas that included champagne and ice cream.

Ceard was engrossed in the menus. 'I'm moving in,' he whispered to me. 'This is my type of tea shop.'

I played along. 'What about your salon?'

'Tell them not to expect me back anytime soon. There's a stock of hairspray in the cupboards and enough gel to last them until the autumn. But if McBride can make chocolate Christmas cakes and Yule logs as luscious as his cream sponges and fudge cakes I'm hunkering in until after Christmas. Wish them Happy New Year from me.'

A tall, stunning looking man, immaculate in a three–piece suit, glared at us overhearing the latter part of our conversation. His aquamarine blue eyes questioned if we knew that New Year was months ago.

We ignored him. Well...that's not strictly true. I may have pulled a face at him. Shame on me for being silly but I didn't like the snooty look he gave Ceard.

'Nice suit,' Ceard said loudly so that the man could hear as he walked away. 'Shame about it showing up the flakes of dandruff on his collar and lapels.'

There wasn't any dandruff in the man's well–cut, light brown hair. Ceard was just winding him up.

The man's shoulders juddered, but Ceard and I pretended to be chatting about something or someone else and moved over to the counter where the chocolate cakes of our dreams were on display.

'Hold me back,' Ceard muttered to me. 'The aroma of chocolate is breaking through my resistance to behave in an adult manner and not wolf a dollop of that chocolate fudge topping.'

'Who is going to hold me back?' I said, eyeing the chocolate–dipped strawberries and ice cream.

'If you jump, I jump,' Ceard said, and then we burst out in a fit of giggles.

'You can take us nowhere,' Ceard admitted, pretending to frown at our silliness.

'When I think about it, perhaps some of my misbehaviour is due to being friends with you.'

'Step away from the patisserie,' said Ceard, 'before we're both lured to the dark side of chocolate and ice cream lusciousness.'

We behaved ourselves for a few minutes, then amid the people milling around, I saw Brodan. He turned and looked at me, sensing he was being watched, or sensing I was there.

Before we went over to him, Ceard pulled me back. 'Does he know about you? Has he been warned?'

'Warned about what?' I said.

'That you're always up to mischief.'

'I am not.'

'And that you tell little white fibs with a straight face.'

'I don't go looking for trouble,' I said.

'But it manages to find you.'

I nudged Ceard, telling him to keep quiet as Brodan approached us.

'Jayne,' he said, smiling at me. 'I'm pleased you could make it tonight.' He eyed Ceard.

'This is my friend, Ceard. He owns a hair salon nearby.'

They shook hands but I sensed tension between them.

'Jayne tells me you're a master at baking cakes and scones,' said Ceard.

'What else did she tell you?'

The question threw Ceard and he blurted out something that made me squirm with embarrassment.

'She said that you're out of her league.'

I kicked Ceard. Half subtle, half couldn't give a hoot if anyone saw me kick his shin.

Ceard winced and then realised he'd done what he had a habit of doing — opening his mouth and letting loose with something that he had no business revealing.

The sound of Ceard back–peddling was loud and clear. 'What I meant was...Jayne wanted me to do her hair so that she looked lovely this evening. Not that she's trying to entice you.'

Just. Shut. Up. I felt like throttling Ceard. Losing my friend and trusty hairdresser was a small price to pay for saving face in front of Brodan. Ceard would've been as well saying — Jayne fancies the pants off you so I did her hair to make her look gorgeous.

I thought Brodan was more embarrassed than me. But I'd yet to learn what his thoughts were when the muscles in his jaw tightened into a firm grin. 'Jayne is already in a league of her own,' he said. 'You look beautiful in your vintage dress. I appreciate that you made the effort to dress for the occasion.'

Brodan certainly had. He wore a suit of such class and quality that I estimated it cost more than I earned in a month.

'Love the suit,' Ceard told him. 'Bespoke is it?'

'My friend is a bespoke tailor. He owns a gents tailoring business in town. I buy my suits from him whenever I can.' He glanced around, searching for him. 'Fergus is here tonight. I'll introduce you.'

I'm sure that Brodan wasn't insinuating that Ceard needed a new suit or that his current suit was tawdry but Ceard wasn't keen to have his menswear attire scrutinised by a top–notch tailor.

'That's fine,' said Ceard. 'We'll have to try out some of your tempting patisserie. That chocolate fudge cake is calling my name.'

'I'll find a seat for you at one of the tables and you can have tea and sample any of the cakes. There's champagne and plenty of tea.'

'Any really chewy caramel confections?' I said to Brodan.

He frowned. 'Yes, there are chocolate caramels and toffee truffles that are particularly chewy.'

'Are they the type that knit your jaws together and make it difficult to talk nonsense?' I asked Brodan.

Brodan smirked and nodded.

'Can we have a plate of them for Ceard please?' I said, indicating that I wished he'd shut up and that I wasn't responsible for what came out of Ceard's blabber mouth.

'I can take a hint,' said Ceard, and wandered off to the cake display leaving me to chat to Brodan.

'That was embarrassing,' I said.

'Did you really tell him that I'm out of your league?'

'Maybe, but it's true.'

Brodan stepped closer and his hazel eyes deepened as he gazed down at me. 'Would you ever consider having dinner with a man who had lied to you?'

'What did you lie to me about?'

'I cancelled our dinner meeting, not because of business, not because something had come up, but because I kept thinking about you in that red suit and the way your blue eyes looked at me genuinely trying to help me with my business by giving me a contact to hire staff. And I thought...I can't get involved with anyone, not when I have to get the tea shop up and running.'

'And so you cancelled our dinner, and lied about the reason?'

'Yes, but I'm hoping you'll forgive me.'

'Excuse me, Mr McBride,' one of the male waiting staff, Donel, said, 'but guests are enquiring about the depth of your scones before baking. Do you cut them to a depth of three and a half centimetres or are yours more? I told them that you're the type of man who believes that every half centimetre counts — especially when your scones have to rise to the occasion.'

I snorted.

Brodan glared at me and went with Donel to chat to the customers.

Ceard waved me over to a table for two. A vintage stand had a selection of dainty crustless sandwiches — smoked salmon, cucumber, egg mayonnaise and cress. Slices of Victoria sponge and coffee and walnut cake were on the cake stand, as were scones, pastries and cakes including Battenberg and butterfly cakes. A plate of chocolates, caramels and truffles sat beside the cake stand.

'I'm sorry,' Ceard said as I sat down. 'I should've kept my mouth shut but you know what I'm like. But I back–peddled immediately.'

'Yes, I heard the gears crunch, and so did everyone else.'

'What did Brodan say to you? Your eyes were like saucers. Speaking of which, I love these tea cups and mismatched crockery. I'd love something like this for the salon customers.'

I opened one of the napkins and placed it on my lap. Then, as I poured our tea using the silver tea strainers, I told him what Brodan had said.

'He lied to you? He's toast.'

'White or brown?' said Donel, thinking Ceard was asking for a slice. 'We also do granary.'

'I think I'll stick to the cakes,' said Ceard, trying not to cause extra work for the staff.

Donel glanced at our table. He was tall and slim with a fresh-faced look and brown hair that had a mind of its own. Although he'd gelled it smooth a few strands stood up at the back giving him a cute little cockatoo.

'I'll bring you our clotted cream and selection of preserves,' said Donel. 'I recommend the raspberry jam with the plain scones and damson with the fruit scones. We've also got vanilla ice cream interchangeable with the cream or just as an added luxury.'

'I'd love some ice cream,' I said.

'Me too, if it's not too much bother,' said Ceard.

'No bother at all, Sir.'

An ice cream display was set up beside the main counter. We saw Donel put a small scoop of vanilla, strawberry, chocolate and a pale green ice cream on little vintage dishes.

'I thought you'd like to try our pistachio,' said Donel, serving up our ice cream. 'Mr McBride grinds his own nuts.'

Ceard winced and went to comment but I glared at him to keep his mouth shut.

'This looks delicious,' I said to Donel.

Donel smiled politely and then hurried to attend to another table of guests.

'Don't look now but the snippy suit is being seated at the table next to us,' Ceard whispered.

Snippy suit's blue eyes flicked a glance at me as he was seated within chatting distance of our table.

He ignored us and we returned the gesture.

All the staff wore name badges. Eila was attending to snippy suit's table. She was very pretty with lovely brown hair that was pinned up in a chignon. She looked harassed and a few of the tendrils had broken loose of the pins.

A couple, a man and woman who appeared to be critical of everything, sat at the table beside snippy suit.

'We're having scones,' the woman said to Eila. 'What's the etiquette? Do we put the jam or the cream on first?'

Eila looked flustered. 'I'm not sure...I always put the jam on first and then top it with cream.'

'That's not what I asked,' said the woman. 'I asked what the proper etiquette is, not what you like to do.' She commented to her husband. 'You'd think they'd hire staff who knew their job.'

Eila's cheeks were bright pink. 'I'm sorry...I...' She tried to apologise but Donal was on the scene like a shot.

'Is there a problem here?' said Donal, glaring at the woman. He knew fine what the issue was. 'Can I bring this to your attention, Madam?' He pointed to a sign for customers regarding behaviour in the tea shop. 'Genteel manners are requested at all times when customers are partaking tea and patisserie in the tea shop.'

Everyone nearby stopped munching on cakes and pastries to hear Donal stand up to the woman.

Her face burned with outrage. 'Are you insinuating that my behaviour is unsuitable for this piddly little establishment?'

Donal shook his head. 'No, Madam. There's no insinuating. I'm telling you straight that if you don't stop being snarky to Eila, you'll be asked to leave the tea shop.'

She scowled at her husband for back–up and at others nearby. There were no takers.

She threw her napkin down on top of her plate of scones and stood up to leave.

Donal cast a parting shot at her. 'And if you're interested in etiquette, never fling your napkin down on the table, Madam. Always leave it to the left of your plate and exit the tea shop as a lady should — politely.'

'I've never been so insulted,' said the woman. 'I'll be reporting your behaviour to the owner of the tea shop. You haven't heard the last of me young man.'

The snippy suit spoke up. 'Give me your name, Madam, and I'll pass on your details to the owner. Brodan is a personal friend of mine. I'm sure I can tell him exactly what happened here.' His tone left her in no doubt that he sided with the waiting staff.

The draft she caused when she left with her husband was swiftly brushed aside as others were eager to find a vacant seat at the table.

Snippy suit caught me smiling at what he'd done. We nodded at each other, two people in agreement that the atmosphere in the tea shop had lightened again.

Donel ushered Eila away and they busied themselves serving customers.

Ceard had been on the verge of speaking up in Eila's defence but had hesitated, worried that he could've cost the young woman her job. I felt the same.

We saw Donal have a word with Brodan who nodded and then went to talk to Eila.

'I think Brodan's assuring her everything's okay,' I said to Ceard.

Donal went by our table.

'Is she all right?' said Ceard.

'Yes, Mr McBride has told her to have a tea break,' said Donal.

Ceard saw her hurrying through to the back of the tea shop. She looked upset and pushed strands of her hair back trying to make herself tidy.

'I'll be back in a minute,' Ceard said to me. 'Her hair's a mess. I'll sort it and be back for another cuppa and a slice of that chocolate fudge cake.'

Ceard went after her.

I was so busy watching Ceard I didn't realise that snippy suit was standing next to me. He extended his hand. 'I'm Fergus.'

Fergus? The bespoke tailor?

We shook hands.

'Brodan tells me you're the one who found this pop–up shop for him.'

'Yes, have a seat. Ceard's sorting Eila's hair. He's a hairdresser. A few wisps out of place and he's got his comb and hair pins out.'

Fergus sat down. The stunning blue eyes were so close that I could see how clear they were.

My heart skipped a few beats. I pushed the reaction aside.

'Please don't let me stop you from enjoying your ice cream,' said Fergus. 'It looks tasty.'

'Would you like some?' Donal offered.

Fergus nodded. 'Thank you. I'll have the same as Jayne.'

He knew my name. He remembered it. It was a small thing but it was nice not to be just the pop–up girl.

'Brodan mentioned that you're a friend of his and a bespoke tailor.' I scooped up some ice cream to calm my senses. What was wrong with me? Overwork. That's what it was. Tiredness played havoc with my emotions. Fergus was handsome in a classic, gentlemanly sense.

'Yes, we've been friends since university.'

Fergus looked to be around the same age as Brodan and only a few years older than me.

'I'm originally from Edinburgh, then I moved to London and opened a shop there while learning other aspects of the tailoring trade. Now I've moved back up to Scotland. I opened a tailoring shop here a year ago.'

'That explains the gorgeous suits. Both you and Brodan look like...'

Do not say they look like tailor's dummies. Do not.

Fergus waited on my description. He knew I was going to say something silly.

'You look very classy. I love a man in a well–cut suit. Sometimes it's sexier than if he wears less clothes. Or casual clothes.'

He smiled and I think I heard him laugh lightly. I was too busy trying not to blush. 'What I mean is — men look handsome in suits. At least some men do.'

My face was as pink as the strawberry ice cream. I put a spoonful of it in my mouth to shut myself up.

He smiled. 'Thank you, Jayne.'

What a sexy smile. He'd hidden it behind the snippy expression. Now I was in the full glare of its power. My stomach tightened and all sorts of wicked thoughts shot through my mind.

Donel served up Fergus' ice cream — scoops of vanilla, chocolate, pistachio and strawberry ice cream.

'Can I bring you a fresh pot of tea?' said Donel.

'Yes, that would be great,' I said.

Fergus looked around the tea shop. 'This was a first–class choice of location for the tea shop.'

'Brodan's really created the atmosphere of an old–fashioned tea shop. The cakes and this ice cream are delicious. I think the shop will be popular especially during the summer with the tourist trade but the locals are sure to enjoy the range of traditional cakes and baking. I know I do. And Ceard wants to move in.'

'I know how he feels. I've always been drawn to traditional things. That's why I love bespoke tailoring — and shops like this.' He looked at my dress. 'Is that vintage you're wearing?'

'Yes, I bought it from a second-hand clothes shop that sells preloved vintage fashions.'

'It's very attractive.'

I blushed at the compliment. He was meaning the dress but I had a feeling that he was including me.

Chapter Three

Ice Cream Cake

Ceard emerged from the back of the tea shop shortly followed by Eila. Her hair was now sorted into an attractive up–do. I saw her thank him and then she busied herself attending to the tables again while Ceard blinked when he noticed that Fergus was sitting in his chair.

Fergus got up to give Ceard his seat back.

'So we're all friends now are we?' said Ceard as I introduced them.

'It appears so.' Fergus smiled at us and then went back to his table.

'Fergus is the bespoke tailor who makes Brodan's suits,' I whispered to Ceard.

'He seemed quite taken with you.'

'Fergus was just being polite. He knew I'd arranged the pop–up shop premises. Besides, you were fussing over Eila's hair. You've made a lovely job of it.'

'She was upset. She was worried she'd lose her job and said that she's been with the catering company who hire out staff to the likes of this shop for several months and needs the work. Jobs aren't easy to find these days. She's working part–time while training to be a patisserie chef.'

'Brodan seems to be fine with what happened, and Donel takes no nonsense from awkward customers.'

'I like Donel's attitude. He's training in bakery work while working all the hours he can get with the hire company.'

I knew how that felt. I'd had numerous jobs and taken training courses to better my prospects while working in restaurants and cafe bars to make ends meet. The pop–up work was my first venture into owning my own business.

Donel brought us a fresh pot of tea and topped up our cake stand with more cakes. I'd finished my ice cream and helped myself to a butterfly cake. The light vanilla sponge, raspberry jam and buttercream icing looked scrumptious. I went to bite into it and then hesitated. 'Is there a particular etiquette to eating it?'

Donel leaned down and whispered. 'Just get your teeth into it and enjoy.'

I laughed and did as he suggested. 'This is delicious.'

'You should try the ice cream cake. I'll bring you a slice,' said Donel.

Ice cream and cake? The perfect combination.

As Donel went away Eila came over to our table. She put a piece of chocolate fudge cake down in front of Ceard.

'I saw you had your eye on this when you came in,' she said to him. 'It's been very popular. I didn't want you to miss out.'

He smiled up at her.

I got the impression the cake wasn't the only temptation Ceard had his eye on.

'Thanks again for doing my hair,' she said and then went to serve ice cream to a busy table.

A slight commotion was caused followed by cheers and laughter as two large bottles of pink champagne were opened by Brodan. He poured them into numerous glasses on silver trays and these were handed out to customers while the bubbles were still sparkling.

Donel brought our champagne over and a slice of strawberry and vanilla ice cream cake for me.

Ceard lifted his glass and clinked it against mine. 'Cheers,' he said.

'Cheers. Here's to a sparkling summer and new beginnings.' The bubbles tickled my nose as I took a sip.

In that moment the atmosphere in the tea shop was as perfect as I would've hoped. Light laughter, chatter, tea cups being filled with tea, cakes and ice cream being enjoyed amid the company of likeminded people who wanted to find something traditional and lovely on this mild May evening.

I looked out the window. The street lights illuminated the people going by, some venturing inside, though it was invitation only. But eager customers were welcomed inside anyway and I liked seeing the joy on their faces when they stepped into the tea shop — like another world where people had time to relax and enjoy a little bit of indulgence.

And I noticed the spark of attraction between Ceard and Eila. She glanced at him a few times while serving other customers.

'She's very nice,' I said to him sipping my champagne and eating the ice cream cake. The layers of strawberry ice cream and luscious vanilla with the light sponge cake were delicious.

'She is, isn't she?' he murmured, and then bit into the rich fudge topping on his chocolate cake.

We smiled at each other and I wondered when he'd ask her out. Before leaving no doubt. Ceard never hesitated when it came to something he was interested in.

But then we saw Brodan slip Eila a card, presumably a business card with his number on it. She held it and looked up at him clearly taken aback by whatever he'd said...or suggested.

'Did Brodan just hit on Eila?' Ceard asked me. I heard the disappointment in his tone.

'It looked like it, didn't it?'

'It did. She seemed surprised, like a woman who thinks he is out of her league.' He gave me a knowing look.

'Yes,' I said, thinking that's probably the expression I'd had when he asked me to have dinner with him.

I was watching Brodan and trying to figure him out when I sensed that I was being studied.

I looked and there was Fergus watching me, watching my reaction to Brodan's move on Eila.

Suddenly the tea shop felt crowded and the genteel atmosphere that I'd been enjoying disappeared as surely as Ceard's chocolate fudge cake.

I felt the urge to get up from the table. I put my napkin down, on the left hand side of my plate. Donel would've approved.

Ceard assumed I was going to the loo, which I was, but only because I wanted to think without Fergus' gorgeous blue eyes looking at me as if I was about to make a mistake. Had I judged Brodan all wrong? Was he a player? If anyone knew him it would be Fergus. Friends since university? Oh yes, Fergus would know the true merit of Brodan's character.

I ran the cold taps and washed my hands, letting the water calm my senses. Any calm lasted only a couple of minutes because Eila came in and wanted to speak to me — girl talk.

'I'm sorry to bother you, Jayne, but I wondered...is Ceard seeing anyone...?'

I blinked. The question rattled around jarring my senses. She'd asked politely. She'd done the right thing. So why did I feel so pressured?

'Ceard is single,' I managed to say. I heard the tightness in my voice. She mistook it for jealousy.

'Oh, I'm sorry. I didn't know that you were interested in him...' She was quick to retract her words but again, she'd done nothing wrong.

'We're friends. Just friends. Friends for years.' How many friends did I need to fit into my reply? I sounded like a demented twit.

She smiled. 'I'd better get back to helping Donel.'

I didn't blame her for disappearing. I'd have done the same. I hurried after her.

'Eila,' I called to her in an urgent whisper.

She stopped and looked round. 'Yes?'

'Did Brodan just make a pass at you? Did he give you his number so you could call him?' I didn't mince my words. Girl talk code made allowances for this.

She bit her lip and nodded. 'He says he wants to chat to me, privately, and wants me to call him to arrange to have dinner.'

I got the message. Some women would've been flattered to be asked out on a date, clandestine or otherwise, by a man like Brodan McBride. However, Eila's reaction wasn't ecstatic. In fact, I think he'd put her in an awkward position. She really needed her job, the work with the hire company. If she refused to have dinner with Brodan would he feel thwarted and inclined to have her replaced? And what would the hire company think? And if she did take Brodan up on his romantic offer, what would that lead to except a brief affair? Or would they have a future together?

So many questions battled each other inside my mind. By the time any answers formed, Eila had hurried back out into the tea shop arena to help Donel. Brodan had hired a few staff for the evening and they were kept constantly busy.

I went back over to Ceard. I sat down and sighed. We'd been friends for too long for me to attempt hiding how I felt. I told him what happened.

'She's not interested in Brodan?' There was hope in his voice.

'She certainly doesn't seem to be. But I think he's put her in an awkward position.'

'I'll bet that's not the only position Brodan wants to put her in.'

'Ssh! Someone will hear you.'

'Someone did,' said Fergus, taking us aback. He stood behind me and was wearing a coat over his suit. 'Luckily, it was just me.' He put a business card down on the table and said to me, 'If you'd like to chat and have afternoon tea sometime, here's my number. And I'm not hitting on you.' He smiled. 'Even though I am tempted.' He nodded acknowledgment to both of us and then left the tea shop.

'And to think I only came in for cake and a natter with you,' said Ceard. 'This makes my gossip of no consequence in comparison.'

We finished our tea but I felt unsettled.

'I think we need to get out of here,' I said.

Ceard stood up. 'So do I, but give me a moment. I want to talk to Eila.'

He went over to her as she cut into one of the large fruit cakes at the main counter. Whatever he said, and I was taking a fair guess that he was asking her out, she smiled and nodded.

Ceard escorted me out of the tea shop. I breathed in the mild evening air.

'That was intense,' I said. 'I feel quite wound up about things. Everything was going so well. I really enjoyed the cakes and ice cream.'

'The pistachio was particularly tasty. Definitely worth Brodan grinding his own nuts.'

'I'd like to grind his nuts for him if he's playing around. What he does with other women is his business, but why was he flirting with me, asking if I'd forgive him and all that smarmy nonsense earlier?'

'I'm buzzing with too much sugary treats to give you a definitive answer. We'll sleep on it. I'll call you tomorrow. We'll have lunch. If we're busy, come over to the salon and we'll have a working lunch, but we'll definitely chat, okay?'

'Okay.'

'Are you having dinner with Eila?'

'Yes. I invited her to go out with me and she said yes.'

I sighed and said what I often said to Ceard. 'Why can't all men be as straightforward as you?'

He smiled and gave my shoulders a squeeze. 'Don't get caught in any webs that Brodan or Fergus are weaving.'

'You think Fergus is cut from the same cloth as Brodan?'

'Just hedging my bets. I think Fergus is okay, but there's something about Brodan that rubs my follicles up the wrong way.'

He walked me to the door of my flat which was further along the main street. His hairdressing salon was at the opposite end of the street.

'What was the gossip you wanted to tell me?' I said.

'You know that I'm planning a secret salon hair evening next week? Invitation only.'

'Yes, but everyone knows about it. Mrs Sherry told me when I met her in the main street that she's baking the scones, fairy cakes and tea bread.'

'You can't keep secrets in this town. You know what the gossipmongers are like.'

I did. I'd been the topic of gossip and been a spreader of juicy stories, so I could honestly see the gossipmongering from both perspectives.

Ceard looked along the street to see that no one could overhear him. 'Mrs Sherry joked about hiring a half–naked man for the evening to give the women a comb through. And a wee thrill.'

'You're not going to give them a bouffant in the buff are you? Your dingle–dangles could get sizzled on your hot tongs.'

'No, of course not. But word got out and I've had a local man apply to do it.'

'Do I know him?'

He laughed and nodded. 'Big MacNeil.'

'Big MacNeil? He's huge.'

'In more ways than one according to his sales pitch for the vacancy.'

'What did you tell him?'

'I wasn't in the salon when he popped in. I was at the bank, getting change for the till, so he spoke to the women, including Mrs Sherry. They told him he'd be perfect, so now I've got a half–naked man as part of the evening.'

'What are you going to call your promotion night now? Fairy cakes and beefcake along with a shampoo and set?'

Ceard laughed as he walked away. 'See you tomorrow, Jayne.'

I went into my flat, hung my vintage dress in the wardrobe and got ready for bed. As always, I brought my laptop with me to check for messages. There were a few that I dealt with quickly. And then I noticed that there was one message from Brodan McBride. The subject heading read: What happened?

I read the brief message: *Jayne, you left so suddenly with your hairdresser friend. Was there something wrong? Call me.*

I typed a reply: *Thanks for inviting me to the tea shop evening. We had a lovely time and I wish you well with your tea shop.*

I pressed the send button before I changed my mind and was tempted to ask him why he'd flirted with me and Eila.

The email disappeared into the ether along with any hope of having anything other than a business relationship with Brodan.

I closed the laptop and breathed a sigh of relief. Juggling all the different pop–up premises and clients wasn't easy. I had to keep on top of the lease dates, prepare the agreements and constantly keep an eye open for new premises. But there was nothing quite as complicated as romance.

Chapter Four

Shortbread & Stealth

I had lunch with Ceard in the little room at the back of the salon. Ceard kept an eye on the clients while eating the filled rolls and snack lunch I'd brought. We were both busy and an easy lunch in the salon was ideal.

Mrs Sherry was under one of the hairdryers so she couldn't hear us talking about her. Mrs Sherry was a trim woman in her early fifties, divorced for years and had never remarried after her husband left her.

'Mrs Sherry isn't happy that Brodan McBride has opened a tea shop and not asked her to bake her special shortbread and scones for him. She's small scale in comparison to him. She's a home baker who makes a bit of pin money from her baking. But her nose is out of joint,' said Ceard.

'Her shortbread is lovely. Crumbles in the mouth. But Brodan bakes his own cakes and scones or hires people to help him.'

'Mrs Sherry is going to apply for a job at the tea shop. However, she's really going in under cover to suss out the competition.'

'Should we warn him?'

'No. He's the newcomer. I'm not ratting her out.'

'I wasn't suggesting we clipe on her. I'm just trying to avoid what will surely be trouble.'

Ceard shook his head. 'We promised not to interfere with things.'

I sighed. We did.

'She came into the salon to have her hair titivated. Code name for having the silver blended into the brunette.'

'I want to look younger,' Mrs Sherry called to us.

We exchanged a look. How did she hear us?

'You look lovely as you are,' Ceard assured her.

'I want to look like I've still got some steam under my bonnet,' she shouted.

Judging from the number of rollers in her hair she was determined to glam things up.

'She asked for an extra ruby glow along with the chestnut rinse,' Ceard whispered. 'I tried to talk her out of it...'

We both knew that this was futile.

'Fiery red could suit her,' I said.

'I've got the pale complexion and bone structure to carry it off,' she called over to us.

Her hairdryer pinged and Ceard went over to check that she was ready for her brush through. He took out one of the rollers and looked at her new colour. 'Dazzling, darling. You are fired up and almost ready to go.'

'I thought I'd go along after lunch when McBride is serving afternoon tea. I want to see his cream scones and cakes. I've heard he's got quite a selection.'

Ceard finished titivating Mrs Sherry's hair. He gave it a lavish spritz with the hairspray and she was set to go.

We watched her from the salon window. Dressed in her coat and carrying her bag, she headed for the tea shop.

'Do you think Brodan will give her a job?' I said.

'She's got her mobile set to stun if he gives her the bum's rush.'

'I guess our money is on Mrs Sherry.'

Ceard put the kettle on for another cup of tea and I told him about the email from Brodan.

'What did you tell him?'

'I told him we had a lovely time and wished him well with his tea shop.'

'So you gave him the brush–off?'

'I just didn't really tell him anything.'

'I don't think a man like Brodan will let things go between the two of you. Especially after he's had a dose of Mrs Sherry.'

I had another cuppa with Ceard and then left the salon. I walked past the tea shop on the way to my flat and couldn't resist having a nosey through the window.

Mrs Sherry had her coat off and appeared to be working behind the counter. Most of the tables had at least two people enjoying afternoon tea.

The sun was quite bright and I had the overwhelming notion for a delicious ice cream cone. One of those classic vanilla cones dripping with raspberry sauce. The salad rolls I'd eaten for lunch had filled a gap but something sweet would've been lovely.

I must've paused too long at the window, lost in thoughts of ice cream cones, because when I blinked, Mrs Sherry was waving at me frantically to come inside. She'd seen me. I couldn't pretend that the sunlight shining off the window had prevented me from noticing her waving desperately.

I went in, trying not to disturb the atmosphere or draw attention to myself. I assumed Brodan was through the back. He wasn't in the front of the tea shop. Donel was serving customers and smiled when he saw me.

I nodded acknowledgment and went up to the counter to talk to Mrs Sherry.

'Mr McBride's given me a try out. I didn't expect him to give me a job. I'm bringing in some of my shortbread tomorrow for him to taste and later this afternoon he's challenged me to a scone–off.'

'A what?'

'Not exactly a scone–off,' she said. 'More like...I've got to bake a batch of plain scones in the tea shop kitchen. If they pass his taste test, I'm hired on a part–time basis.'

'And are you okay with that? I mean...' I kept my voice to a whisper, 'you only came in to suss out his patisserie.'

'I know, but I think it's my hair. It takes years off me.'

The way the sun was streaming through the front window and catching the highlights in it she looked like she was on fire.

'Tell Ceard ruby and chestnut are my colours from now on.'

'I will.' I glanced around. 'I'm going to dash before Brodan sees me.'

'Sees you doing what?'

I turned and there was Brodan staring at me.

I couldn't think of a plausible excuse. I couldn't even think of a ridiculous excuse and I'm adept at that, or so Ceard says.

'Sees Jayne indulging in another slice of your fantastic ice cream cake,' said Donel, sensing that I was floundering. Yes, I definitely liked Donel.

Two large hands gently guided me to the nearest table and sat me down. 'I insist that you indulge,' said Brodan. 'It's one of those warm May days when ice cream cake goes down a treat.'

The only words that rang in my head were — *May* and *days*, though as my mind panicked I translated it as the distress signal — mayday, mayday.

If Ceard could see me now. I'd wanted to avoid Brodan and here I was being cajoled into eating his ice cream cake. Okay, so there are worse things than strawberry and vanilla sweetness, but my heart was racing just being near Brodan. What if he invited me out to dinner, again?

Before I could think of an excuse, Brodan smiled at me. 'So, when are we having that dinner?'

'Well...I...eh...'

'What about tomorrow night? If you're not busy.' He smiled as he said this and looked normal. It was easier when I thought he was being a two–timing twister.

'Sorry, I'm busy. I'm having dinner with...' Come on brain, think of someone. It couldn't be Ceard. He was having dinner with Eila. If Brodan did fancy Eila I doubted he'd want to make up a foursome.

The hazel eyes gazed at me. 'Dinner with...?'

I blurted out the first name that shot into my mind. 'Fergus.'

'Fergus?' he said. 'Right, well, have a lovely evening with him.'

The noise of an oven pinging in the kitchen made him hurry away to attend to his baking.

Mrs Sherry cut up slices of Battenberg and raised her eyebrows at me as Brodan dashed past her into the kitchen.

'He looks like he's had the puff knocked out of his souffle,' said Mrs Sherry.

'He did, didn't he?'

'And is Fergus that tailor? I've heard about him and seen him in the street, but I've not spoken to him.'

I nodded.

I thought about making a run for it but Donel smiled as he served up a slice of ice cream cake.

'I gave you a slice with two fresh strawberries and some raspberries on it,' he said.

I didn't have the heart to leave, so I smiled and began to eat the cake.

All was calm for a few minutes. Brodan stayed in the kitchen allowing me time to eat my cake.

Now that I'd lied about having dinner with Fergus while eating yet more delicious tea shop delicacies courtesy of Brodan, who should walk into the shop but Fergus.

I had two choices. Three if hiding under the table was allowed, which it wasn't. That left two choices. Keep eating my cake and pretend everything was fine or admit that I'd lied.

Unfortunately, Mrs Sherry ruined any hope of these when she saw Fergus.

'Come on in. There's a seat beside Jayne. I'll get another cup and pot of tea for your table.'

Fergus was pleased and sat opposite me while Mrs Sherry fussed around us. 'Where are you having dinner?' she asked him.

He frowned and smiled. 'Eh...at home.'

'Oh, so you're cooking dinner for Jayne? How romantic. I love a man who knows one end of a frying pan from the other.'

Fergus looked at me. The stunning blue eyes questioned what was being said. Had he heard right?

'Dinner at your house,' I said. 'I'm really looking forward to it.'

Mrs Sherry hurried to get our pot of tea while I was left with Fergus.

I ate a morsel of ice cream cake. 'This is delish.'

Fergus leaned closer across the table and said quietly, 'Was I the most plausible excuse you could come up with? Because I'm assuming someone, possibly Brodan, asked you out and you used me as a buffer.'

My cheeks burned as pink as the strawberry ice cream. 'Yes, and yes.'

He leaned back. 'If you're not interested in Brodan then what are you doing here? Apart from scoffing ice cream cake.'

'I've been asking myself the same thing.'

'Any answers spring to mind?'

I nodded. 'It was an accident.'

'You accidentally walked in here, sat down and ordered cake?'

'Nearly. Tweak a few minor things and that would explain it.'

He smiled as Brodan came out of the kitchen carrying a fresh batch of scones.

'Your turn,' he said to Mrs Sherry.

With a confidant flick of her bouffant, she went into the kitchen.

Brodan piled the scones on to a cake stand in the display cabinet.

A couple of customers pointed to the fresh baked scones and requested one while they were still warm from the oven.

While Donel and another member of staff served up the scones and dealt with customers, Brodan busied himself at the cake counter, arranging the display and cutting wedges of cake for the staff to serve.

He nodded and smiled to Fergus but didn't approach our table.

'Did Brodan ask you to have dinner?'

'Yes,' I said to Fergus, explaining the predicament.

Fergus broke his scone open, spread jam on his scone and then added cream on top. 'I suppose I'll have to cook dinner for us.'

'No, you don't have to do that.'

'We can't go out for a meal. People will think I've burned the dinner.'

'We don't need to have dinner together. I'll hide out, I mean, I've got a lot of work to do at home. No one will know I'm not having a romantic meal at your house.'

Fergus shook his head. 'Someone always knows. In this town, there are few secrets.'

I nodded.

'Can you cook?' I asked him.

'Yes.'

The doubt in his voice was loud and clear.

'But I'm not in Brodan's league. I'm more basic. Oven chips and pizza. Maybe some salad thrown in. Are you okay with that?'

'It sounds great.'

'My house at seven?'

I didn't even know where he lived.

'Do you live in the town?' I said.

'I do. My house is the large one with the shutters overlooking the sea.'

'I didn't know that anyone lived there. I don't usually walk that far along the shore at this time of year.'

'I only moved in before Christmas. You can drive down. Take the esplanade road. You'll see a turn off for my house.'

I stopped eating my cake and sighed.

'I'd finish that cake if I were you. Brodan is watching.'

'I'm sorry I've caused you this bother.'

'No bother, Jayne. Who knows...maybe our dinner date will be better than either of us think.'

'The chips could be golden and crispy and the pizza cooked to perfection.'

'And a blue moon in the sky could shine off the sea.'

We smiled at each other and I picked up my fork to finish my cake.

The following day was a flurry of viewing new shop premises, contacting clients and paperwork. But in the back of my mind I kept thinking about having dinner with Fergus.

I finished my paperwork at the flat, closed the laptop and got ready for dinner. The evening was warm and mellow as I drove down to Fergus's house. The sea shimmered along the coast and I rolled down the window to breathe in the fresh air. I'd dressed smart but casual — trousers and a top in creamy tones and a light blue cardigan. I kept my hair down and my makeup natural. I didn't want Fergus to think that I considered our dinner to be a date. It was only the outcome of circumstances and a stupid lie that we'd both decided to follow through on.

I saw the lights on inside the large two–storey, white–painted house and parked in the driveway. The front door was open and I wandered into the hallway that lead to a spacious lounge with a large fireplace. The fire was unlit but lamps lit up the room which was expensively and elegantly furnished.

Opposite the lounge was a staircase and further along the hall I heard someone busy in the kitchen.

'Fergus?'

'In here, Jayne.'

I followed the voice and tried not to laugh when I saw Fergus making dinner. His kitchen was well–equipped and he'd set the table near the window with plates, silverware and wine glasses. He looked like a quintessential gentleman in his bespoke clothes and so out of his depth trying to handle a tray of crinkle–cut oven chips.

He thrust the tray in my direction. 'Do these look ready to you?'

They were pale golden. Very pale. 'I'd give them another few minutes.'

The chips were put back in the oven and the pizza pulled out. His lovely blue eyes looked for my approval.

'The pizza seems ready. Do you want me to help serve it up?'

The relief showed on his face. 'Would you?'

I took my cardigan off and put it over the back of a chair and set about helping Fergus organise dinner. For two people who didn't really know each other we worked well together and soon dinner was on the table — golden chips, slices of cheese and tomato pizza and a green salad.

I made us a pot of tea and skipped the wine. So did Fergus.

'You've got a lovely house and garden.' I peered out the large window at the lawn and patio area. The kitchen was at the back of the house. The front had a view of the sea.

'It's a bit big. Four bedrooms, two bathrooms, a huge lounge that extends out the front when the glass doors are open. It belonged to a client and he went to live abroad so I snapped up the property as an investment.' He glanced around. 'I enjoy my privacy and it's great that it's right on the edge of the seashore, but sometimes I feel like I'm the only person around.' He smiled at me. 'It's actually quite a novelty to have dinner with someone...someone like you.'

'Surely you must have friends round. Girlfriends and so forth...'

'I dine out if I'm with friends. Cooking isn't my thing. As for girlfriends, I haven't had one of those since I moved here. I've been too busy and haven't met anyone special. What about you?'

'I'm not involved with anyone at the moment. Like you, I'm busy.'

'The things we do for our businesses, eh?' he said.

'I thought I knew most of the businesses town but it's quite a busy town. I don't think I've seen your shop.'

'It's tucked up one of the cobbled lanes. I don't need a main street location. My customers find me wherever I am and I prefer being in a niche away from the main hub. You should come and visit when you have time.'

I smiled and nodded.

'Apparently this house used to be a hive of activity during the summer in its heyday. It was used for entertaining and part of the sailing events, fairground attractions, parties and dances. The front lounge is huge and large enough for social dances. Do you dance?'

'I'm as adept at dancing as you are at cooking. But I enjoy afternoon tea and cake.'

We finished our dinner and took a tray of tea and biscuits through to the lounge. The windows stretched from the floor to the ceiling. I wandered over and gazed out at the long sweep of the sandy bay, the islands far off in the distance no more than misty silhouettes on the waterline.

Fergus opened the doors and let the sea air waft in. There was barely a breeze — one of those mellow early summer evenings. He brought a small table over and we sat there on two elegant chairs sipping our tea.

I felt myself relax. I gazed out at the sea. 'I could get used to this.'

'You're welcome to pop down anytime. I'm usually here. Well, not in the lounge exactly, but working away in the study. I bring my work home with me most evenings.'

'The bespoke tailoring work?'

He stood up. 'Yes, come on, I'll show you.'

I put my cup of tea down and followed him through to the room across the hallway. It was a smaller version of the front lounge and had the same view of the sea, but it was kitted out like a sewing study with a large desk lit with a lamp, a cutting table, two tailoring mannequins, clothes rails filled with suits, jackets, trousers and gentlemen's attire, and stacks of fabric on shelving. Another table had a paper pattern pinned to a classic dark fabric, the makings of a suit I assumed. Tailor's chalk, measuring tape and various accoutrements for his bespoke work sat where he'd left them, probably to make dinner for me.

'I love fabric,' I said, going over to the selection that ranged from light grey to charcoal, stone to moss green, ecru to chocolate, navy to the deepest inky blue. I didn't touch any of it. I imagined every finger mark could ruin the perfection he so obviously created.

'Do you make any clothes for women? Business suits? Skirt suits?' Oh how I would've loved one, not that I could've afforded it.

'No...well...I did make a ladies waistcoat once for someone I used to date.' The tone of his voice hinted that he'd really loved her. 'She said it was her favourite item and wore it until it was almost threadbare. She worked in the city, in finance, and said it always made her feel great.'

'Threadbare? You must've dated her for a long time.'

'Two years. The waistcoat was still like new when we parted. She moved away. We'd started to drift anyway so when she was promoted we called time on our relationship.'

'But she kept in touch?' She must have if he knew she'd worn it until it was almost threadbare.

He nodded. 'Up until last year when she got married. We don't keep in contact now. Our past is in the past where it belongs.'

'Is that why you moved here to the coast to get away from the past?'

'No, I've always loved to sail. I own a yacht at the marina and go out on it whenever I have the time, especially in the summer. But no, clients of mine had moved here and I grew to love it more than the city. So I moved. I prefer the pace of life here. It's far more hectic.'

'More hectic?'

'You've lived here a lot longer than me. Surely you know what this town is like. Gossipmongers and stirrers thrive. There's always something going on. Look at us. In the city I'd be having dinner in one of my favourite restaurants or relaxing in the house I used to own there. Instead, I've been running around juggling oven chips and a pizza, worried I'd left the plastic base on it after I'd put it in the oven. And harassed wondering if there was any way that part of you wanted to have dinner with me and that we weren't just playing out a date because you'd told Brodan you were having dinner with me.'

Phew! It all came out in one blast.

Car headlamps lit up the window and the sound of a car pulling up sharply in the driveway interrupted us.

Fergus looked outside. 'It's Brodan.'

Brodan didn't use the front door. He came in through the lounge and headed straight to the study.

'Is something wrong?' said Fergus.

'Yes. My manager up in Glasgow has just quit. I have to head up there to deal with the business tomorrow. But I can't be in two shops at the one time so I came to ask a huge favour of you.'

Fergus nodded.

I looked at Brodan. I'd never seen him look so out of sorts. Seeing Brodan and Fergus standing together I realised how similar they were in height and build. Although Fergus was leaner, this evening Fergus was the stronger of the two.

Brodan took a deep breath. 'I need your help, Fergus. Can you hold the fort for four or five days while I sort out things in Glasgow? I've phoned Donel and Mrs Sherry. They've agreed to come in full-time to keep the tea shop running. I've dropped the shop keys off at Donel's house. He'll open up early in the mornings and start the baking along with Mrs Sherry. Eila will come in too and work extra hours. But I need someone to deal with the money, the takings, the banking.'

Fergus was already nodding. 'I'll handle that for you. We both use the same bank for our business. I'll have a word with the manager but you'll need to authorise me to do this.'

'Can I draft up something here?' Brodan looked at the laptop on Fergus' desk.

Fergus typed up a brief letter and printed it out.

Brodan signed it. 'I'll phone the bank in the morning to confirm what we're doing.' He put a set of keys on the desk. 'And could you check in on my parents' house over the weekend?'

Brodan kept glancing at me. I wasn't sure what that look was in his gorgeous hazel eyes. A look of goodbye? Surely not. Brodan would be back in a few days. Wouldn't he?

Chapter Five

Champagne Afternoon Tea Party

'This doesn't affect the pop–up agreement, does it?' Brodan asked me.

'No, and I obviously understand the circumstances.'

He nodded and I thought he was going to say something to me but then pressed his lips into a firm line.

A flash of guilt shot across his handsome features. What was he hiding? I sensed it wasn't to do with the pop–up lease. He'd paid all the money in advance so it wasn't as if he was reneging on the payments. What was the problem?

'I'll help Fergus and the others in the tea shop when I can,' I said.

Brodan smiled. 'Thanks, Jayne. I've got two party bookings, so any help then would be welcome.'

'What type of parties?' I said.

'A hen night tea party. It should be bedlam. The women are dressing up in forties vintage dresses. It was booked last week. One of them came in while I was setting up the shop. They're into vintage and asked if I'd organise an evening for them. It's basically a champagne afternoon tea menu but it starts at seven in the evening until ten. Donel says he's capable of handling the women.'

'I'm sure Donel is a whiz in the kitchen but I don't know about handling a room full of party girls,' I said.

'Fergus will keep them entertained, won't you?' said Brodan.

Fergus laughed. 'What have I got myself into?'

'There's a similar evening, but it's a birthday party. A friends and family affair. I've already iced the birthday cake.'

It seemed like we could handle the tea shop parties. Couldn't we?

'I'm heading up to Glasgow now,' said Brodan. 'Thanks for your help. Sorry to have interrupted your evening.'

'Would you like a cup of tea before you go?' said Fergus. 'There's plenty left in the pot.'

'I don't want to intrude.'

'Nonsense.' Fergus brought the tea tray through from the lounge into the sewing study. He put it down on the edge of the desk and ran off to the kitchen for an extra cup leaving me alone with Brodan.

I was going to ask him if there was something he wanted to tell me but he began extolling the merits of Fergus' tailoring.

'That's my new suit. I'm having it made for the tea shop.' One of the mannequins was wearing the work in progress. He went over and showed me the details. 'It's got some real old–fashioned styling on the lapels and a top pocket for a handkerchief.'

'It's ideal having your suits made–to–measure.'

Brodan gasped. 'Don't let Fergus hear you use that phrase. You'll never be invited to dinner again.'

'What phrase?' Fergus arrived with another cup and poured our tea.

Brodan explained my faux pa. 'Fergus creates suits from a pattern that he makes personally for each customer. Basic templates aren't used and then altered to fit. Oh no. Everyone has their own pattern. His bespoke suits are all handmade from top quality cloth.' He looked again at the suit. 'I love the cut of this.'

'Have you got time for a fitting?' said Fergus.

Fergus unbuttoned the jacket, slipped it off the mannequin and held it up without giving Brodan a chance to refuse. He smoothed the shoulders and checked that the length of the sleeves was just so and that it sat well when buttoned across Brodan's chest.

'I've made so many suits for Brodan over the years that I can usually gauge it right unless he's been overworking and lost weight,' Fergus explained to me.

'It's a beautifully–cut classic jacket,' I remarked.

Fergus wheeled a full–length mirror over from the corner. 'What do you think?'

Brodan studied his reflection and nodded his approval. 'Perfect. If only life ran as smoothly as the finish on this worsted fabric.'

'Try the trousers on.' Fergus picked a pair of trousers from a hanger on the rail. 'If they fit I'll have the suit finished by the time you get back next week.'

Brodan hesitated and looked at me.

'Oh, okay,' I said, realising they wanted me to avert my eyes while Brodan took his trousers off and put on the other pair. I tried not to look at Brodan's reflection in the mirror. I really did try. He had strong legs. Not that I was looking...ahem.

Fergus adjusted the trouser hem, pinning it so that it was perfect.

Brodan took the trousers off carefully so as not to mess with the alternations and put his own trousers back on.

'You can look now,' said Fergus. 'He's decent, or at least as decent as he can manage.'

Fergus hung the trousers back up on the rail and that's when Brodan realised that I must've been able to see him in the mirror. My blushing cheeks helped give the game away.

Brodan smiled at me and said nothing. But he knew. Oh yes, he knew.

After giving Fergus other details about the tea shop, Brodan got ready to leave. We walked with him outside to the car.

'Don't worry about things,' Fergus assured him. 'Jayne and I will hold the fort.'

'Thanks again.' Brodan's gaze was directed at me. And there it was again — that flicker of...I wasn't sure. Guilt? Goodbye?

I was still wondering about it as his car drove off along the shore road. Fergus stood beside me.

'Is there something Brodan isn't telling me that I should know?' I asked him.

'Perhaps, but it depends on how you feel about Brodan.'

'Tell me.'

Fergus' blue eyes gazed out at the sea. The night had deepened and moonlight reflected off the water.

'Brodan's manager...' Fergus began.

'What about him?'

'Brodan used to date her.'

'Oh.'

'When he agreed to move down here for a few months, she wasn't happy about his decision. It's no secret, and in this town it's bound to make its way along the gossip grapevine, but Brodan had a stormy two–year romance with Keriann. They split up recently, before he agreed to look after his parents' house, but I think she hoped they'd give their relationship one last chance. With Brodan moving away, she'd warned him she wouldn't wait around for him coming back. I guess she quit altogether. She'd often threatened to leave the business.'

'Brodan seemed particularly stressed when he arrived. Does he still have feelings for her?'

'I don't know, and I don't think he does either. But maybe when he realised she'd actually gone he knew how he felt about her.'

Something in my heart changed as he said this. That's what I'd seen in Brodan's expression. He was still in love, even just a little, with his ex. But he certainly didn't seem like he wanted to be. Maybe he'd settle things between them or he'd finish their relationship. I wasn't sure and I don't think Brodan was either.

Fergus laughed and jolted me out of my doleful thoughts.

'What's so funny?'

He pointed out at the sea. The trick of the light as the moon shone on the sea made me smile.

'A blue moon,' he said. 'Not in the sky but in the sea.'

'It still counts.'

He nodded. 'I didn't burn dinner.'

'You cooked a tasty dinner.'

Now all we had to do, apart from our own work, was run the tea shop. Mrs Sherry could bake up a storm so I had no worries there. I only hoped that Donel was as adept as he seemed to be otherwise we'd be relying on Fergus not burning the scones. And although I was an expert at munching cakes, I definitely wasn't skilled at baking any.

'Can you bake?' said Fergus.

'Not even a muffin or a crumpet.'

'I quite enjoy a bit of crumpet.'

I smiled. 'Don't look at me when you say that.'

'I was gazing out at the sea,' he said and then laughed. 'And searching for another blue moon. I think we're going to need one.'

Donel opened up the tea shop. I had a meeting to view one of the shop premises further along the street so I peered in the window and gave him a friendly wave.

He wore a chef's hat and whites and a determined expression. He waved back and beckoned me in.

'I'm up to my eyeballs making pink macarons for the hen party. They've insisted on them. I need an honest taster.'

I was hauled inside the tea shop and a pale pink macaron filled with strawberry buttercream was thrust at me. It was barely eight in the morning, but I've never been one for refusing cake or confectionary just because it's the wrong time of the day.

Mrs Sherry had her flowery apron on and was busy sorting out the cakes. 'Donel's ruffled edges are brilliant.' She sounded impressed.

I wasn't a macaron connoisseur but apparently smooth macarons with ridges around the edges was the mark of a bloomin' great macaron.

'Mmmm, this is exquisite,' I said.

He straightened his chef's hat. 'I aim to please.'

Mrs Sherry was at the counter putting fondant tea roses on top of the vintage cake for the party. Pastel fondant bunting decorated the edges of the tiered masterpiece.

'Wow! That looks beautiful,' I said.

'Brodan baked the cake and covered in it smooth royal icing, but Mrs Sherry's sugarcraft skills are handy for creating the finishing touches,' said Donel.

'Are you coming to the party to help out?' said Mrs Sherry.

'Eh, yes. And so is Fergus.'

'It should be a lively night,' said Mrs Sherry. 'I know a couple of the girls. They were going to book the party at one of the restaurants but were told that hen party attire such as fairy wings and wobbly headbands that flash in the dark weren't allowed. Brodan says they can wear whatever they want. They're dressing up in vintage clothes — polka dot dresses, tea dresses, and matching their fairy wings and hen party accessories to those.'

I left Donel and Mrs Sherry to get on with their baking. I walked along the main street towards the prospective new shop premises. A bright blue sky indicated that it was going to be a lovely warm day and I could feel a bit of heat in the sunlight.

The morning flew in and at lunchtime I dropped by the hair salon to see Ceard. I had sandwiches, yoghurt and fruit with me, enough for the two of us.

'Is it that time already? Where did the morning go?' he said.

He put the kettle on for the tea and we settled ourselves in the back of the salon for a quick lunch and a chat.

'I've been doing a few of the women's vintage hairstyles for the party tonight at Brodan's tea shop. Another five women are due in this afternoon.'

'I promised I'd help out at the party.'

'Do you want an up–do? I've got some vintage–style clasps.'

'I'm not even sure what I'll be doing at the tea shop tonight except running around serving customers and keeping mayhem to a minimum.'

'I'll sort your hair.'

While the kettle boiled Ceard pinned my hair up, securing it with pins, setting lotion and vintage clasps.

'Thanks.' I shared the sandwiches between us and Ceard made the tea.

'These sandwiches are yummy,' said Ceard. 'Did you make them?'

'Yes, I think Brodan's tea shop is getting to me. I bought a few extra items with my shopping this morning. I thought I'd make Scottish cheddar sandwiches with red onion marmalade.'

'Very nice. So what's happening with the tea shop? How long is Brodan away?'

I told him everything.

'Brodan's manager is his ex–girlfriend?'

I nodded.

'It sounds like he still holds a candle for her.'

'I think he does.'

Two women came into the salon and one of Ceard's assistants welcomed them in.

'That's two of the hen party guests,' said Ceard, knowing we'd have to cut our lunch short and get on with our work.

I left him a tub of yoghurt and some fruit. 'If you're not doing anything tonight, drop by the tea shop. I need all the back–up I can get.'

He gave my up–do a lavish dose of hairspray as I was leaving the salon. 'That'll keep it from unravelling.'

'If only it could do the same for me.'

'Brodan's tea shop isn't your worry,' Ceard whispered.

'I know, but I'm responsible for the pop–up hire, and Donel and Mrs Sherry are hoping that I'll help them.'

'Fergus is helping though, isn't he?'

'He managed not to burn the oven chips last night but he's a tailor not a chef or a baker.'

The women were giggling and chattering excitedly about the party.

Ceard looked at me. 'I'll be there at seven if only to ensure the girls behave themselves. But if Fergus is useless in the kitchen, you'd better put an apron aside for me.'

I kissed him on the cheek. 'Thanks, Ceard. See you tonight.'

I wore a blue cotton dress and smart but comfortable black pumps for running around in the tea shop.

Donel and Mrs Sherry had everything set for the party when I arrived. They'd strung extra bunting up to add to the vintage theme. Champagne glasses shone on the white linen table cloths and the silverware was polished to perfection. Fairy lights lit up the main counter and music from yesteryear played softly in the background.

The shop smelled of baking — fresh bread, cakes, scones and hints of strawberry and lemon with notes of spices and chocolate.

'We're all set,' said Donel, looking spruce in his chef's whites.

Mrs Sherry adjusted the angle of the tea rose cake on the main table. 'We've baked and made everything that was ordered. Lots of sandwiches, coffee and walnut cake topped with coffee frosting and pieces of walnut, and fairy cakes with chocolate liqueur.'

'It looks fantastic,' I said. It really did.

'I've made steamed pudding — a syrup and jam sponge and plenty of custard,' said Donel.

'And we've got champagne and jugs of cocktails,' added Mrs Sherry.

I checked the time. Five minutes to seven.

'Here they come,' said Donel hurrying over to unlock the front door.

I heard them before I saw them. Chatter and raucous laughter invaded the cosy atmosphere of the tea shop.

The girls looked great all done up in their forties and fifties finery, with their hair and makeup to match the era. Several of them wore sparkly fairy wings. The atmosphere notched up into the party zone as their hearty laughter and energy filled the tea shop.

Donel disappeared for a few moments as the girls hugged and kissed him, thinking he was the owner. I'm sure he meant to tell them otherwise, but when he emerged, his face adorned with bright red lipstick kisses — and one on his chef's hat, he was the most delighted I'd ever seen him.

He seemed to float rather than walk through to the kitchen to attend to the food, while I tried to look like I knew what I was doing serving up the tea, cake and sandwiches.

'Keep the cake stands topped up,' Mrs Sherry said to me. 'I'll start serving up sandwiches. And champagne.'

One of the guests smiled at Mrs Sherry as she served their table with glasses of champagne. 'I love your vintage makeup.'

Mrs Sherry blinked and put a hand to her deftly powdered face with its pink blusher and matt red lipstick. 'What vintage makeup?'

More women arrived and we were rushed off our feet.

'Where's Fergus?' Donel hissed.

'I don't know,' I told him.

Mrs Sherry sneered. 'He's probably chickened out.'

I refilled one of the cake stands with Victoria sponge and scones, and eagerly peered out the window. There was no sign of Fergus, but then I saw Ceard hurrying along the street.

I unlocked the front door and let him in. We'd decided to keep the door locked so there would be no issue with party crashers.

The women cheered when they saw Ceard and I barely had a chance to talk to him because he was grabbed and pulled into their midst. While they chatted about the fabulous hairstyles he'd given them, and advised some of the other women how to achieve similar styles with hairpins, gel and large rollers, I tried to keep up with Mrs Sherry and Donel.

Eila arrived around seven–thirty straight from one of her patisserie training courses and got stuck into the task of serving the tables with tea, champagne and plenty of scones.

Ceard's face lit up when he saw her and there was definitely quite a bit of flirting going on between them. This of course didn't go unnoticed by the hen party guests who teased Ceard and Eila.

Fergus arrived an hour later wearing one of the most stylish suits I'd seen him wear. The women's interest perked up when they saw him. He did look handsome, and an unexpected stab of jealousy went through me as they shifted their flirting from Ceard and Donel to Fergus.

'I love your suit,' one of the girls said, feeling the fabric on his jacket.

'Is this your tea shop?' another woman asked him.

'No, it belongs to a friend of mine. He's away on business.'

'What is it you do?'

'I make suits. I've got a tailoring shop in the town.'

'Do you make women's clothes?' one of them asked.

He smiled. 'No, just clothes for men.'

She gave him a sexy smile. 'That's a pity. I'd have popped into your shop for a personal fitting anytime.'

'Behave yourselves,' Ceard told them.

One of them stole Donel's hat, put it on and gave him a smacker of a kiss. 'We are behaving ourselves, Ceard. Aren't we, girls?'

A roar and cheer went up.

Fergus didn't know what to do when it came to serving the women.

'Maybe I should leave,' Fergus said to me. 'I'm useless at this catering malarkey.'

'You can boil water and make more tea,' I told him, 'or take your jacket off, roll your shirt sleeves up and make yourself useful clearing the dishes. Donel is up to his elbows in the kitchen. He needs a hand.'

As Fergus took his jacket off, raunchy cheering and whistling erupted. The women were winding him up.

Fergus hurried into the kitchen. It was the fastest I'd ever seen him move.

Donel came out carrying a delicious sponge pudding and put it down on the table beside the counter. 'Anyone want some roly–poly?' he announced.

One of the women laughed. 'I wouldn't say no, Donel. And I'll have a portion of that sponge pudding too.'

Donel blushed but he was loving every moment of it.

I doubted the evening would've been as cheery if Brodan had been there. Maybe things had worked out better like this.

As the laughter, chatter and happy atmosphere swirled around me, I looked at Ceard and Eila smiling at each other, at Donel beaming that so many women were flirting with him whether it was light–hearted or not. I got the impression that Donel had never been the centre of female attention like this before and was relishing it for all it was worth. Having lost his hat during the proceedings, the little tufts of hair that usually stood up were nothing in comparison to his current hairstyle. For the past two hours numerous women had run their hands through his hair and now it resembled a prize cockatoo, but he didn't seem to mind. Ceard tamed it for him twice, but within minutes the women's playful hands had ruffled it again.

Then I saw Fergus, sleeves rolled up, revealing his strong, lean forearms. The top buttons of his shirt were undone. He'd taken his tie off but kept his silk–backed waistcoat on. It emphasised his broad shoulders and trim waistline. A wave of excitement went through me. Fergus wasn't just handsome, he was sexy, and the only woman he seemed interested in that night was me.

Chapter Six

Fondant Tea Roses & Birthday Cake

The women filtered out of the tea shop around ten o'clock, extolling the virtues of their champagne tea party. Several of them had placed orders for cakes — for birthdays, various celebrations and a couple of them just because they loved the traditional iced sponge with fondant fripperies.

They were heading to a nightclub to continue their evening and had taken Donel with them. Well, we assumed they had. They'd been threatening to steal him as we wrapped up the tea party, and although Donel said he would help with the clearing up we hadn't seen him since he'd been near the front door taking down some of the extra bunting. When the taxis drove off, Donel had completely disappeared. Somewhere on a nightclub podium a chef dressed in his whites, with cockatoo hair, was dancing the night away with a group of wild but happy women.

I flicked the lights off upstairs in the tea shop and for a moment I peered out the windows. The street was quite busy with traffic and revellers, and in contrast the sea looked calm, glistening along the shore.

I was so lost in thoughts that I didn't hear Fergus come up the stairs and approach me.

'Ceard's made tea,' he said over my shoulder. 'Come and have a cup before we lock up for the night.'

I looked up at Fergus. His blue eyes looked so clear in the light from the streetlamps shining in the windows. And his lips, smiling gently at me, were so close that if I'd been inclined I could've kissed him.

'Great,' I said, deliberately jarring myself so that I didn't do anything foolish like kissing Fergus on impulse. It had been a long but cheerful night and I was still buzzing and yet feeling exhausted at the same time. A dangerous cocktail of emotions, especially as Fergus looked so damned handsome standing there.

I saw a flicker in the depths of those gorgeous eyes of his. Had a similar thought crossed his mind? Or was I reading romance into things that weren't really there?

I'd been holding my breath and let a sigh slip from my lips as I went to go past him and down the stairs.

'Jayne,' he whispered, and pulled me back into a passionate embrace that took us both by surprise.

Fergus kissed me with more passion than I'd experienced in a long time. This man could kiss. I gave in to the moment and let myself melt into him.

When he let go of me we stood there gazing at each other.

'Are you going to slap me?' he said, worried that he'd overstepped the mark.

No, I was far more tempted to wrap myself around him and go for another passionate kiss. But I restrained myself.

'Blame the champagne,' I said. 'I may have had a couple of glasses of bubbly and some of Mrs Sherry's cocktail mix during the evening.'

'Thank goodness for the champagne and cocktails,' said Fergus. 'If it wasn't for them, we'd have to admit that we're attracted to each other. And that would never do, would it?'

I shook my head and smiled at him. Fergus was flirting with me and I did nothing to thwart him.

'Tea's ready,' Ceard shouted up the stairs to us. 'I hope you two aren't canoodling up there.'

We hurried down trying not to look like we'd been up to mischief, but I'd forgotten that I'd refreshed my lipstick and that the evidence was there on Fergus' lips for everyone to see.

'Woo–hoo!' said Eila.

I blushed and tried not to laugh.

Fergus stirred sugar into his tea, smiled and looked suitably embarrassed.

'You make a lovely couple,' said Mrs Sherry.

'It was just a goodnight kiss,' I told her. 'The party atmosphere spilled over and we got caught up in the moment. Isn't that right, Fergus?'

'Whatever you say, Jayne.'

Everyone burst out laughing which made the atmosphere light–hearted.

Ceard put his arm around Eila's shoulder. 'Maybe there's something in the tea and cakes that encourages romance,' he suggested to us.

Mrs Sherry gave him a look. 'Ahem!'

'Okay, but the night's not over yet. I'm sure there's some man out there for you, Mrs Sherry.'

As if to remind us all of the forthcoming salon party, MacNeil swaggered past on the other side of the street with some friends. He waved over to the tea shop when he saw us lit up near the front window.

We waved back.

Ceard winked at Mrs Sherry.

'Not on your nelly,' she told him. 'Me go with big MacNeil? It'll never happen. There would have to be a blue moon in the sky.' She untied her apron and put it in her bag.

'We saw one of those last night, Mrs Sherry,' said Fergus. 'Didn't we Jayne?'

I nodded. 'We did indeed, so you'd better keep a tight grip on your pinny,' I told her. 'Ceard's salon parties are renowned for their mischief and mayhem.'

We appeared to have ruffled Mrs Sherry's feathers, but I wasn't entirely sure she didn't like flirting with the notion of an amorous evening with the hot–blooded kiltie. He'd told us he was wearing his kilt and like a true Scotsman, he was going commando.

Having finished our tea and established that Mrs Sherry was definitely not interested in what was under MacNeil's sporran, we locked up the shop, gave the keys to Mrs Sherry to open up the next morning and headed off into the night.

Ceard walked Eila home. Mrs Sherry hurried along to her wee house beside the sea, so that left me with Fergus. We paused at the door of my flat.

'I live upstairs, above this shop,' I said.

'See you tomorrow night.'

'Yes, the birthday party sounds less chaotic, but I'll be glad when Brodan gets back and we can all relax into our own lives again as normal.'

'There's no such thing in this town, Jayne. Only variations of trouble and misbehaviour, but I wouldn't change it for the world.'

'Neither would I,' I agreed with him.

He hesitated, on the brink of a kiss. His mouth was a breath away as he murmured, 'I'd kiss you goodnight but I guess I should behave myself.'

I smiled up at him. 'In a town like this?'

Without letting me say another word he pulled me into his arms and kissed me. If anything, our second kiss was better than our first. I could've sworn it lasted a minute but I'm sure it was only a few seconds. He smiled and walked away towards the seaside road that led to his house.

I watched his tall silhouette disappear and wondered what would happen when Brodan came back. Would that change everything again? And did I want it to?

I slept sound — from exhaustion, sheer hard work, exhilaration and excitement thinking that we had another tea party to organise the following night. I fell asleep thinking about kissing Fergus and wondering where all this would lead.

Light rain washed across the main street the next day, but by the evening the weather had become one of those warm, muggy nights, so I wore another little cotton dress and my comfy pumps and headed to the tea shop. I'd pinned my hair up myself. The style was no match for the one Ceard had given me the previous night, but it was fine.

Fergus was already there. I saw him talking to Mrs Sherry inside the tea shop that was all lit up again ready to entertain the birthday party guests.

Colourful balloons replaced the extra bunting and Donel was tying two of them to the blue bicycle outside the front window. He gave me a harassed smile when he saw me.

'I'm all out of breath blowing up these balloons,' Donel huffed. 'I thought they'd be easier to stick up than the bunting.'

'The balloons look wonderful.'

He stepped back to admire his handiwork. 'They do, don't they? Very cheery.'

We went inside.

Fergus smiled at me and I thought about him kissing me the previous night. Would this evening end with warm, summer kisses? A surge of heat flushed across my cheeks.

I went over to the counter to see what the birthday cake looked like. 'Oh very nice,' I said.

'Brodan iced it,' said Donel. 'It's a married couple in their thirties who are having the party for family and friends tonight. It's the wife's birthday. She's into all things vintage so he organised this for her.'

As we spoke, the guests started to arrive.

'Here we go,' said Mrs Sherry.

Fergus unlocked the door and we welcomed everyone in. They were a happy crowd but subdued in comparison to the hen party. The tables were set with white linen and silverware again but tea lights in coloured vintage glass holders were lit in the centre of each table. The tea shop looked so pretty.

'I've snapped some photographs to show Brodan,' Fergus told me. 'I thought the tea shop looked especially lovely, as do you by the way.'

I blushed.

He leaned close. 'I hope you don't feel awkward with us having...kissed.'

'No,' I lied.

He gave me a knowing smile.

Donel carried the birthday cake through to the main table.

Fergus dimmed the shop lights as the candles were lit on the birthday cake. The little lights on the tables added to the atmosphere as the cake candles were blown out and wishes made.

Fergus turned the lights back up.

Champagne toasts, speeches, cheers and gifts were enjoyed by the party guests.

I topped up one of the cake stands with Battenberg, crustless finger sandwiches, slices of chocolate truffle cake and Earl Grey tea scones.

'My wife made the curtains for the windows upstairs,' the husband confided to me.

'Really? I love the patterns — cakes and ice cream.'

He was pleased to tell me about his wife running a sewing and craft business from home. 'Brodan McBride read her advert in the local newspaper and asked her to sew the curtains for him. She suggested the fabric,' he explained. 'Someone said that you're the pop–up girl,' he added. 'My wife's thinking of expanding her wee business and maybe getting shop premises. Do you have a number where we can call you to arrange a chat?'

I went through the back and got a business card from my handbag and gave it to him.

'I'll give you a call soon,' he said.

'I'll have a look through my portfolio and see if there are any low–cost pop–up shops that would suit your wife. A couple of new shops became available this week.'

'Sounds great. We'll get together and have a chat, Jayne.'

I went through to the kitchen where Eila was showing Ceard how to serve up slices of the ice cream cakes. Mrs Sherry had made her classic vanilla ice cream and they'd used that for the layers of ice cream and sponge cake. Mrs Sherry made the smoothest, creamiest ice cream that I'd ever tasted.

'Add strawberries, raspberries and whipped cream to the vanilla cake slices and cherries to the chocolate version. The salted caramel ice cream cake is served as it is,' Eila said to Ceard.

'What if someone just wants an ice cream cone?' he said.

'Give them a cone and offer extras such as dipping the cone in chocolate or adding raspberry sauce and sprinkles,' she told him.

Ceard set about slicing up two large ice cream cakes — one strawberry and vanilla and one chocolate. 'We're postponing our dinner date,' he said to me.

I'd forgotten he'd asked Eila out to dinner. 'I'm sorry, Ceard,' I said.

'No problem,' he assured me. 'We've been getting on fine working together in the tea shop. We've been flirting over the patisserie.'

I took a tray of clean tea cups out to the tables. Donel was explaining to some of the guests how to make a perfect cup of tea and how to serve it... 'Pour the brewed tea into the cup and then add the milk. You need to see how strong the tea is, so pour it first and then pour the milk or add a slice of lemon. And never both. Never, ever have milk and lemon.'

The guests tried out Donel's techniques for using a tea strainer and pouring without splashing tea on to the white linen table cloths.

A couple of the guests stirred their tea and Donel winced when he heard their teaspoons hit off the sides of their cups. 'Never rattle your spoons around. Swish the teaspoon back and forth and fold the milk and sugar in. Teaspoons should be seen but never heard. Noise during tea should be kept to a polite minimum.'

The swishing commenced and Donel nodded his approval. 'That's the way to do it.' And then off he went back to the kitchen.

'Are you doing anything tonight?' Fergus said to me.

'Apart from serving tea, cake and ice cream?'

He smiled at me. 'I mean later, after we've finished up here. I thought perhaps you'd like to come down to the house and enjoy some sea air and a cuppa with me.'

I hesitated, knowing where his offer could lead.

'No pressure, Jayne. It's just that this is the first night in months that I've not been at home working. I thought that it would be lovely to have your company. Honestly, it's just for tea.'

I smiled up at him. 'Nothing else?' I teased him.

'Maybe a sandwich and a bit of cake if there's any left after the party. We could take it with us. Then I'd only have to make the tea and I think I can do that especially after hearing Donel's tea tips.'

'And never put a dirty spoon back into the sugar bowl,' Donel said on passing. 'Always use a clean spoon.'

Fergus nodded firmly at him. 'Noted.'

We thought he'd gone but he stepped back into the kitchen. 'I'll put some cheese and tomato chutney sandwiches aside for your smoochy date later on.'

'What smoochy date?' I called after him, trying not to laugh and blushing like mad. 'And speaking of smooching, Donel, what about you disappearing last night with the hen party girls? What happened? We want details.'

'My lips are sealed,' he called back to me.

'They weren't sealed last night,' I said to him. 'You were enjoying every minute of those women kissing you.'

He smiled and hurried on.

'There's definitely something in the tea in this shop,' commented Mrs Sherry. 'All this romance and smooching. It's even getting to me. Last night I found myself lying in bed, by myself of course, rethinking my attitude on big MacNeil. I had to get up and make a cup of cocoa.'

Once the guests had gone and we'd all tidied things up, Fergus and I were the last to leave the tea shop. Ceard and Eila had headed to the dancing taking Donel with them.

'What about you, Mrs Sherry?' I said to her.

She put her chiffon scarf on. 'I'll be glad to put my legs up when I get home and indulge in two cups of cocoa.'

Fergus checked that all the things were switched off and in the semi–darkness we headed to the front door. I had a bag full of sandwiches and cakes. Fergus had insisted on paying for them.

He took a last look around. 'I guess this is it then.' He sounded wistful. 'I didn't think I'd enjoy working so hard at something I have no talent for, but I've had two of the most exciting and enjoyable nights in ages.'

'There will be other tea party nights.'

He shook his head. 'Not like this. Brodan will be back. We won't be needed.'

'We'll have our own party night,' I said without thinking it through.

'Like a tea dance party?' He sounded enthusiastic so I didn't like to backtrack on my impulsive suggestion.

'Yes. A tea dance. I'm not sure where.'

'At my house. There's plenty of room. The lounge floor would be ideal for dancing. It'll be great to have the house filled with people. I always feel as if I'm rattling around in there in my own little world. It's about time I had a party.'

So with the semblance of a plan for a tea dance, involving Brodan's tea shop as part of a promotion, if Brodan wanted included, we drove down to the shore to have tea, sandwiches and cakes at Fergus' house. And no smooching. Definitely, absolutely none.

That was the plan. But most of my plans never, ever worked out.

Chapter Seven

Tea By The Sea

We sat in the lounge with the front patio doors open having our tea, cake and sandwiches.

The night air wafted in as I poured another cuppa for us from the teapot. We'd been chatting about the tea dance.

'A summer tea dance would be ideal,' said Fergus.

'A great excuse for me to buy a dress.'

'A tea dress.'

I pictured wearing a classic flowery dresses. 'I've got one of those hanging somewhere in my wardrobe. I might not need to buy a new one. I bought it last summer from one of the pop–up shops I was dealing with. It's gorgeous and a real bargain. I'm not sure it'll still fit me. I've lost a bit of weight since then.'

'I'd be happy to alter it for you. Bring it with you the next time you're here,' he said as if I was going to be a regular visitor.

'I thought you didn't handle women's clothes,' I said lightly.

'I'll make an exception for you.' This had a deeper meaning. The only other woman he'd made or altered clothes for had been very special to him. He held my gaze and my stomach fluttered with excitement.

I took a deep breath of sea air, letting it cool my senses. 'It's getting late. I should get going.' I put my tea down and stood up. I knew that if I stayed any longer I might end up spending the night with Fergus, and I wasn't ready for that. Jumping into relationships wasn't my style.

'I'll drive you home,' he insisted.

It was only a couple of minutes drive up the road. He parked the car outside the entrance to my flat.

'Any plans for tomorrow?' he said.

'I'm viewing a new pop–up premises. I'm also hoping to catch up on all my paperwork and emails.'

'Give me a call if you'd like to have dinner one evening.'

I could see that he was trying not to pressurise me and I liked that.

'At a restaurant,' he added. 'I promise not to do any cooking.'

I smiled and nodded, and then as I went to get out of the car he kissed me. A brief but passionate kiss. And of course that's when someone saw us smooching. MacNeil gave us a raunchy cheer and waved across at us. He was with a couple of friends going home after a night out.

I acknowledged MacNeil with a quick nod, got out of the car, waved Fergus off and hurried inside my flat.

I got up early and went to the nearby shop to buy fresh baked morning rolls and tattie scones for my breakfast. Mrs Sherry was in the queue along with MacNeil. She was trying to avoid his gaze, but when he saw me he had no hesitation in letting everyone know that he'd seen me kissing Fergus.

'Are you going steady with that suit man?' he called over to me. 'You were fair snogging him in the car last night.'

'You're exaggerating,' I told him.

He laughed and pointed at me. 'I saw you. Your lips were glued to his. Did you invite him up for a coffee?'

'No, he drove straight home.' I hated having to explain, but from experience I'd learned that ignoring remarks led to more speculation and gossip. It was better to deal with them as if I had nothing to hide.

'Were you kissing Fergus?' Mrs Sherry whispered.

'It was just a goodnight kiss.'

She smiled. 'I quite like him. But I've often thought that you and Ceard would end up together. You get on so well with him. And Ceard's lovely.'

'Ceard's great but we've been friends too long for us to be anything more than that.'

The queue moved along and thankfully MacNeil got served and left the shop. He gave me a knowing wink as he left.

Mrs Sherry continued to chat to me in whispers. The shop was always busy in the mornings but the rolls were worth the wait.

'I had a relationship like that years ago,' Mrs Sherry confided. 'That was before I got married.' She'd been on her own for a while now and chatted openly about her past. 'We'd been friends since we were at school. We always got on, and he was a fine looking man. Everyone thought we'd end up together but I kept dithering, thinking that we were friends and not wanting to spoil that. But it turned out to be nonsense. I shouldn't have hesitated. It was a mistake I regretted for a long time. I suppose I still do.'

'Did you date him, or were you only ever just friends?'

'I dated him one summer, and then I decided to back off when I got a new job. He went away on a training course and met someone else. He never came back. He married her, so I heard, but someone told me years later that he always said that I was the one he should've married.' She sighed and looked so sad.

'Anyone else got a cheery story this morning?' the shopkeeper announced.

Mrs Sherry put her rolls and a pint of milk on the counter. 'You shouldn't eavesdrop,' she told him. 'Besides, you were moaning last week about your wife canoodling with the postman behind the shop counter.'

'My husband never touched her,' a woman piped up from the back of the queue. 'He was helping her lift a heavy parcel.'

A few people tittered causing further debate about the postman being extra helpful.

We both paid for our shopping and continued to chat outside the shop.

'I hope you do get on with Fergus,' said Mrs Sherry. 'But be careful not to discount Ceard. I know he's having a wee fling with Eila but make your choices carefully.'

'I'm taking my time and not getting involved too quickly with anyone.'

'Have you heard anything about Brodan McBride coming back?'

'No, but Fergus seems certain he'll be here again soon.'

'The tea shop's closed today, but Donel's going in later to bake some cakes. I said I'd pop in and help him. I'll make some of my shortbread and strawberry ice cream.'

'Brodan's lucky that he's got you keeping things ticking over for him.'

'I heard some gossip about Brodan's ex–girlfriend,' she confided.

'What about her?'

'She's a right madam. A snippy wee arse. There's talk that Brodan might not come back to the tea shop. She wants him to stay in Glasgow.'

'But he's got the pop–up lease for the whole of the summer.'

She shrugged. 'I'm just telling you the gossip.'

I sat in my kitchen having a mug of tea and eating my buttered rolls with grilled tattie scones.

I kept wondering what would happen to the tea shop if Brodan didn't come back.

In the afternoon I drove up the coast to view a new shop property, and then headed back as a mellow early evening sun cast a glow over the town.

Upstairs in my flat I looked out at the sea in the distance, shimmering like gold.

I made myself a light dinner of salad and grilled fish. I sat at the kitchen table eating my dinner and gazing out at the seaside view. One day I hoped to own a house on the edge of the sea. I doubted I could ever afford a house like the one Fergus had but there were cottages I had my eye on. If my pop–up business continued to make a profit I planned to rent or buy one of those. In the meantime, I liked my cosy wee flat, especially on evenings like this when the light from the sunset filled the front rooms with a burnished glow and the sea shone in a blaze of glory.

And I thought about Fergus...and Ceard. I'd had a text from Ceard telling me he'd spent the night with Eila and that things were going well between them. He also reminded me that the secret salon evening was looming nearer. I replied that I'd chat to him at the salon. He'd helped me at the tea shop. The least I could do was help him with his promo night, even if I did have to deal with MacNeil and whatever antics he had planned for entertaining the women at the party.

The little pop–up shop was tucked into a select niche in the town. I had an appointment with Isa and Iain, the couple who had the birthday party at the tea shop.

I'd come up with a vacant premises that I thought would be ideal for her sewing business, and had sent them a few details by email. They were interested and wanted to see the shop. The owner was friendly and very flexible on the lease. He'd wished me luck and gave me a crossed fingers gesture as he'd handed me the keys earlier to show them the property. It had a floor–to–ceiling front window that would be suitable for displaying her fabrics.

I got there about ten minutes early, turned all the lights on and pushed a decorating table into the corner to make it as appealing as possible.

Fergus' shop was nearby. I planned to drop in and see him after I'd shown Isa the premises that I thought would be perfect for her sewing shop. Small but affordable.

I hadn't seen Fergus for a couple of days and we'd both been busy, but he'd phoned me the previous evening to let me know that Brodan was due back the next day.

I looked out the window and saw Isa and Iain walking up the street. She was visibly excited, looking at the shop window, grabbing him and gesturing her enthusiasm. He was smiling. It was heartening to see how much he cared about her business and how enthusiastic she was. Moments like these were why I loved my work. There was an energy and excitement to someone starting or expanding a business and it brought new life to empty shops.

I opened the door. 'Come on in,' I said, smiling at them.

Isa ran in ahead of him. Iain smiled as he came in. 'It's nice to see you again, Jayne. Thanks for doing this.'

'My pleasure.' It really was.

They had a look around.

'It's new to the pop–up market,' I said. 'I know it's not on a main street but as you have an advert running in the local paper people will be able to find you. The low cost is a bonus and the owners are very amenable to you being here. You could try it out for the summer, but they said they'd be happy to extend it into Christmas and the New Year. They may even offer you a permanent lease if things work out.'

Isa was already standing there planning her future shop. 'I love it, I love it. I can see how it will look. This wall will have fabric racks. I'll put sewing accessories, needles, buttons and stuff like that in the centre. Thread selection racks on this wall, and my sewing machine and table near the counter.'

It sounds lovely,' I said. 'I can picture ice cream and cake print curtains adorning many of the houses in the town soon.'

They both laughed, and then looked at each other. I could tell they'd already discussed this for a long time and this was a big moment for her.

She looked at him with a wide–eyed grin and gave him a nod.

Iain laughed and interpreted her actions. 'I think that's a yes, Jayne.' He wanted to pay for the five-month lease by cheque upfront.

I smiled and pulled the lease agreement out of my bag.

'Oh, you've got it here,' said Isa, taking a deep breath.

'Yes, the owner said if you decided you wanted it, I can leave the keys with you.'

Well that sealed the deal. Isa signed on the dotted line and I handed her the keys to her new shop.

I left them to take in their premises and phoned the good news to the owner who was delighted to have a happy tenant.

I put my paperwork in my car and then walked along the cobbled street to Fergus' shop. The front window was class personified. Two male mannequins wore exquisite suits and the lighting emphasised the cut and quality of the workmanship. Accessories such as ties, braces, brogues, and other items that a gentleman would require to look well-dressed were part of the window display.

I was so busy studying the display I hadn't realised that Fergus had seen me and was waving at me. He hurried to the door. An old-fashioned bell tinkled when he opened it.

'Jayne, come in,' he beckoned. He seemed genuinely delighted to see me.

My heart filled with happiness.

I stepped inside, into another world, a timeless niche where traditional bespoke tailoring stood strong against the modern world where fashions changed at the drop of a hat.

Quality. That's what hit me. Sheer, beautiful and wonderful quality. And right in the middle of it, standing there grinning at me, blue eyes shining with a warm welcome, was Fergus.

He'd been working at his pattern cutting. He wore a white shirt, silk tie and a waistcoat.

'You've had your hair trimmed,' I said, noticing that his light brown hair was extra smart.

'I've been to the barbers this morning. It's not too short, is it? I told them I wanted it a bit longer than usual.'

For me perhaps? So that I could run my fingers through its silky texture when he kissed me?

'Not too short at all. Very smart. Very handsome.'

The word *handsome* slipped out and resonated in the quiet shop, emphasising it to full effect.

I blushed. 'What I meant is...'

He put his hand up. 'I'll take the compliment.'

I looked around. It was all polished wood, plush carpeting and traditional styling. I loved it.

'Would you like a cup of tea?' he said. 'And biscuits.'

'Lovely.'

He went through to the back of the shop and filled the kettle. A tiny kitchen as immaculate as his front of shop area had space for making tea. He set two cups up — white cups with silver rims, and put a selection of biscuits from a large tin of posh biccies on to a plate.

I stood in the doorway watching him. Every time I saw Fergus he seemed more handsome than the last. Was I falling for this man? Or was I seeing him as I should've done without the shadow of Brodan McBride taking the shine off him? Probably a bit of both.

'I can hear your mind evaluating something. I hope it's not me unless it's all cheery thoughts.'

'I was just thinking...' *That you're gorgeous. Far more handsome than I first thought. You set my pulse racing. Fill my mind with wicked thoughts of how I'd like to kiss you right now.* Forget about the tea and biscuits. I'd have happily settled for a few luscious kisses from the bespoke tailor.

The kettle clicked off and he poured the hot water into the tea pot. 'Thinking what?'

'That I love...your shop.' It wasn't a lie, it was a diversion from the truth.

He smiled at me. Fergus was sharp. He knew I was telling a fib. Did he know how he affected me? Maybe a little bit. Maybe a lot.

I told him about the new pop–up shop.

'A sewing shop nearby will be ideal for trade. Anything that encourages working with fabrics and making clothes and home accessories is great.'

He made my tea the way I liked it — strong with a splash of milk and no sugar. He handed it to me. I helped myself to a chocolate bourbon. Fergus opted for a custard cream.

'Where are you off to now?' he said as we drank our tea together.

'To help Ceard organise his secret salon event.'

'The open secret that everyone knows about?'

'Exactly. It's on tonight at seven.'

'At the salon?'

'No, the venue was moved to Mrs Sherry's house. She's probably up to her eyes in baking her special shortbread as we speak.'

'Is Donel working at the tea shop today?'

'Yes, Donel and Eila. They'll close at five and then Eila is helping Ceard with the party.'

'I heard that MacNeil has a surprise in store for the ladies. Something to do with his kilt.'

I gulped. 'If it involves stripping it off and doing the rumba in his sporran, I think I'll be leaving early.'

'Spoilsport.'

'Are you encouraging me to ogle a half–naked man?' I said lightly.

He gazed down at me with his gorgeous blue eyes. 'Not at all. There's only one half–naked man I'd encourage you to ogle.'

'If someone is getting changed in the fitting room,' a customer called through to Fergus, 'I can come back later, Fergus.'

Fergus's tea cup clattered in his saucer and he dashed out to attend to one of his prize customers. 'No, your booking is scheduled as planned. If you'd care to take your jacket and trousers off in the changing room, I'll get your new suit ready for its fitting.'

As the man disappeared into the changing room, Fergus closed the curtains behind the man and beckoned me to come out.

I slipped out of the shop without the client noticing.

'Phone me later,' Fergus called to me outside the shop. 'Let me know how the salon evening goes. And call me if you need back–up.'

'What for?'

'In case MacNeil and his sporran aren't the only surprise in store this evening.'

'What do you mean?'

'Brodan called me about an hour ago. He's on his way down from Glasgow. He could be at the tea shop by now.'

That seemed like a good thing, so why was I tense? And why was Fergus looking at me as if a ferret was threatening to run up his trouser leg?

'You look...perturbed, Fergus.'

'Brodan won't be alone when he comes back.' He looked right at me as he announced the news. 'He's bringing Keriann with him.'

Mrs Sherry's description shot through my mind. *'She's a right madam. A snippy wee arse.'*

'There could be a clash of personalities if Brodan allows Keriann to manage the tea room. I doubt that Donel will put up with any of her renowned snippiness,' said Fergus.

'Neither will Mrs Sherry.'

'I've a feeling there's going to be trouble. Perhaps you'd like to keep away until the ructions blow over.'

I nodded.

'Should I keep my tie on, Fergus?' The customer emerged from the changing room in his shirt, tie, socks and underpants.

'I have to go. We'll talk later, Jayne.'

Fergus hurried inside to attend to the client and I drove back to my flat. I planned to stop off to warn Donel and Mrs Sherry about Brodan bringing his ex–girlfriend. Or were they now a couple again? I presumed they were. Why else would he bring her down to the tea shop?

But Brodan's car was parked outside the tea shop. I parked opposite when I saw Donel storm out of the shop. Even from this distance the steam pouring from his ears was obvious.

I ran across the street. 'Donel, are you okay?'

We were along from the tea shop and Brodan couldn't see us chatting.

'Brodan's snotty wee girlfriend is calling the shots now at the tea shop,' said Donel.

'Have you quit?'

'No, but I'm sure she'd like me to. I'm leaving early. I told Brodan I'll be back in tomorrow. Keriann complained that the silverware needed cleaned.' He became outraged at such a suggestion. 'I'd worked for an hour polishing it all myself until it was gleaming. She was just being rotten. I was making my fruit scones at the time but Brodan told me to polish the silverware and she took over the scone making. And she ruined them. She put nutmeg in them. Nutmeg! She doesn't have a clue.'

He took a deep breath and I let him continue. 'There's an atmosphere in the tea shop that you could cut with a cake slice. Two customers left early after only having a raspberry tart and a frangipane meringue. Is there anything you can do, Jayne, to sort out that wee shite?'

'I'll see what I can do,' I promised him.

He walked away. I straightened my blouse and skirt and headed into the tea shop. In the distance Donel gave me an encouraging thumbs up.

Chapter Eight

Ice Cream & Scandalous Behaviour

I heard Brodan talking to customers upstairs, but Donel was right. The atmosphere was like tinder. Four tables were occupied with customers who ate their cream teas while watching the fiasco.

Piercing green eyes glared at me. Keriann seemed to know who I was. She'd probably checked me out online and seen photos. I had to admit she had a beautiful face with sharp but perfect features and a lovely pale cream complexion. She was similar in build to me and around the same height. We were both slight figures but she had an underlying aggression about her. The type who liked to pick fights, backed up by her position as Brodan's girlfriend. I disliked women like her who abused their position just because they were nasty wee swines.

I didn't flinch. I think if I had she'd have approached me, perhaps to tell me I had no business being in the tea shop or something equally abrasive.

We glared at each other. No way was I backing down. The noise level in the tea shop went down a few decibels as customers paused from stirring their tea and munching cakes to watch the silent stand–off.

But then the green eyes switched from me and targeted Mrs Sherry who was busy behind the counter adding sprinkles to a strawberry fairy cake. Keriann approached her instead, keeping her voice to a level that Mrs Sherry and I could hear but making it difficult for the customers to decipher.

'I was just telling Brodan,' Keriann began, 'that I think you're perfect for the tea shop, Mrs Sherry. Old–fashioned, from another era.' She sneered at Mrs Sherry's handmade, flower–patterned apron. 'Antiquated.'

Before I could step–in to say something, Mrs Sherry's eyes narrowed and she hissed a warning reply. 'See you, ya wee shite — back off.'

Keriann smirked. 'Or what?'

Mrs Sherry glared at her. 'Or I'll stick this fairy cake so far up your arse you'll be farting sprinkles for a month.'

A few customers almost choked on their tea, but no one complained to the owner.

Keriann thought about retaliating but then she thought better of it. She'd met her match, and they needed Mrs Sherry to keep the tea shop running smoothly, especially as Donel had left early. The look in Mrs Sherry's eyes was fierce. The warning was clear. Don't let the flowery vintage apron fool you. This fairy cake is poised for action.

Brodan came bounding down the stairs. 'Is everything okay?' His eyes glanced between Keriann and Mrs Sherry.

Mrs Sherry smiled tightly. 'Yes, we were just discussing the patisserie.'

Keriann's glossy chestnut ponytail swished in anger and she marched through to the kitchen.

Inside I was cheering. And I think so were the customers.

Everyone continued as if there was no change in the watermark.

Brodan came over to me. 'Can I help you, Jayne?'

I felt like a stranger or someone who'd been dismissed. Any attraction I'd felt for him vanished. No wonder he was involved with Keriann. They were well-suited to each other.

Eila served the customers without any comment, as if she was trying not to step out of line. I understood that she needed the work so it left a bitter taste to see her act like this. I wanted to shout at Brodan, but then I thought better of it. Keriann would've enjoyed seeing me throw a wobbly in the tea shop. I'd look like the troublemaker, not her. So I kept my comments to myself. For now.

'I heard that Keriann was here,' I said, trying to sound friendly. 'I came to invite her to Ceard's secret salon party tonight. She could have her hair done and meet the girls. Get to know everyone.'

Keriann emerged from the kitchen. Perhaps it was the combination of her name and the word party that coaxed her out.

'I'm not sure,' Brodan answered for her.

'Well, if you don't think Keriann should go, Brodan...'

Keriann triggered and took the bait. 'I'd like to go,' she said, overriding Brodan.

In the background Mrs Sherry was glaring at me and her knuckles were white with the grip she had on a butter knife.

'The party is being held at Mrs Sherry's house,' I said.

Keriann's face fell slightly, but I added some icing to the invitation.

'We've got some entertainment for the women, haven't we, Mrs Sherry?'

She managed to smile and nodded.

'Yes,' I elaborated. 'One of the local hunks, MacNeil, is wearing his kilt, but perhaps not for long.' I winked. 'If you know what I mean.'

Keriann actually broke a smile. I imagined the porcelain on her face crack into a thousand pieces.

I smiled at Keriann. 'See you tonight at seven then?'

I went to leave but Brodan said, 'Are men allowed to go to the party?' Was that a hint of jealousy in his tone? Didn't he like the idea of Keriann being let loose for a wild night with the girls?

'Sorry, it's girls only. Apart from Ceard, obviously, as he's the hairdresser and MacNeil because of his...assets.'

Mrs Sherry spoke up. 'Unless you'd like to join in and give us a display of your hidden talents, Brodan.'

Keriann laughed and Brodan scowled but tried to force a smile. 'I'll leave that to MacNeil.' He scurried off to the kitchen.

I left the tea shop. Mrs Sherry hurried after me. 'What were you thinking inviting that wee hellcat to the party?'

'I thought she'd enjoy herself,' I said. 'Besides, Ceard told me that MacNeil wants one of the women to help him get the night started by ripping his kilt off. I thought Keriann could volunteer. It'll be a nice surprise for her. When he twirls her round his head like a caber she'll have a great time, won't she?'

Mrs Sherry nodded and gave me a wink. 'Yes, she's looking a wee bit pale. MacNeil will bring a flush of colour to her cheeks. And I'm not just talking about her face.'

I phoned Ceard and told him about Keriann. He was well up for her being there, especially when I told him how she'd treated Mrs Sherry and Donel and that Eila was walking on eggshells around her.

'It sounds as if it's going to be an entertaining evening,' said Ceard.

'Oh I think it will be hair–raising. In more ways than one.'

I loved vintage, so I automatically loved Mrs Sherry's house. Although most of the items in her house were unintentionally vintage–style, everything from the quaint decor to the chintz curtains had an ambiance of the past. It was one of the pretty cottages down by the sea along from Fergus' house.

As promised, I'd phoned Fergus to give him an update on what was happening. He'd jokingly told me that he was setting up the binoculars hoping to get a glimpse of the chaos that was due.

I wore a pale lemon dress, another second–hand bargain from the shop where I'd bought the tea dress. The evening was warm with a soft breeze. A few people had arrived as I drove up. The sea glistened like silver in the fading light. Yes, I definitely wanted a cottage like this when I could afford it.

The soil beside the sea wasn't ideal for growing flowers, but Mrs Sherry had used a top layer of lush soil and had a magnificent spread of flowers and a strip of lawn.

The sound of women chattering and tea cups rattling in saucers drew me into the cottage. The front room was set up like a salon and she'd arranged the bathroom so that Ceard could use it if he needed to dampen anyone's hair. Generally, it was more to do with styling, using hair accessories, gel, experimenting with makeup and having a laugh while enjoying tea, cakes and champagne. And ice cream. Plenty of ice cream. Mrs Sherry had made vanilla, chocolate and strawberry ice cream. Her freezer was topped up to the brim.

Jugs of her homemade lemonade and limeade were chilling in the fridge. I had a glass of lemonade rather than champagne. I wanted to keep a clear head, and besides, I loved her lemonade. On a hot evening it was refreshing, especially when I accepted a scoop of vanilla ice cream with it. The ice cream fizzled in the tall glass and almost bubbled over. Delicious, totally delicious.

Ceard gave me a hug when he saw me. Eila was with him.
'Where's Keriann?'

'She'll be here,' I told him. And as if to prove me right, she drove up and parked outside. She wore a glamorous little black dress with loads of sparkly sequins. Most of the women had worn light, summery dresses and clothes. Keriann looked like she was dressed for a nightclub, but she did look stunning and I envied her diamante studded high heels.

'Here's Keriann,' Mrs Sherry announced.

Numerous sets of curious eyes watched her walk in. Mrs Sherry welcomed her and introduced her to Ceard.

'You've got lovely hair,' he told her.

She wore it down and it looked like she'd brushed it to a shiny, smooth perfection for the occasion.

'I'd like you to show me an easy way to put it up into a chignon,' she said.

'Take a seat,' he said.

And so the salon event started with Keriann learning how to make herself even lovelier than ever.

'Where's MacNeil?' I whispered to Mrs Sherry in the kitchen while I helped her make more ice cream drinks. The champagne was popular, but the lemonade and ice cream was the favourite, closely followed by a cup of tea and a slice of Victoria sponge.

Mrs Sherry wore a pinny over her dress. She matched the flowery curtains on the kitchen window. 'He's getting dressed in the bedroom.'

I frowned. 'Getting dressed? Did I miss something?' I was sure I'd arrived on time.

'He was rehearsing earlier while I got the house ready for the party.' She busied herself at the sink and tried not to look at me.

I nudged her. 'What were you up to with MacNeil?'

'Nothing.' Her reply was a high–pitched squeal.

'Did he strip off in the living room? Did you get a private performance?'

We tried not to laugh but then broke into a fit of giggles.

'He arrived an hour early on my doorstep,' she said. 'What was I supposed to do? I invited him in. He said he wanted to suss out the lounge to see how much room he had to swing his things around.'

'What things?'

'His things...you know...equipment. He's got his full highland dress including a shoulder cape that he plans to whirl around.'

'And he gave you a display?'

'I was sitting in the living room having my tea. I wasn't expecting him to go all the way. I can't remember eating my baked beans and mashed potatoes but when he'd finished I'd cleared my plate.'

'There's a big, strapping man standing in the hallway, Mrs Sherry,' one of the women shouted into the kitchen. 'He wants to know when to make his grand entrance. And can you put the ornaments off the fireplace in case his swingers knock them off.'

Mrs Sherry immediately dropped her scouring sponge into the sink water and hurried through to the living room.

'Okay, ladies,' Mrs Sherry announced. 'For your entertainment we've got a hot–blooded big kiltie ready to show you what he's made of. If this doesn't curl your hair for you, ask Ceard for his tips on using large rollers and setting lotion.' She clicked the music on. It was loud and beat a fast–paced and rousing rhythm.

A wild cheer went up.

Ceard pulled Eila aside and they stood out of reach at the back of the lounge. The windows were open to let the sea breeze keep the temperature down but nothing was going to dampen the women's ardour when they saw MacNeil leap into the living room.

The floor shook — and so did MacNeil. Oh, but that man could move. In a good way. I think.

I looked across at Keriann. Her eyes were wide and she was actually smiling. Yes, smiling.

MacNeil shimmied across the living room carpet, discarding various items from his attire. His shirt flew over the sofa and was grabbed by two of the women who waved it around like a triumphant flag.

'You'll have to give us a flash if you want your shirt back big man,' one of the women shouted to him.

Without hesitation, MacNeil burled around so that his kilt went up to reveal that he'd kept his word and gone commando. 'Keep the shirt. I'll exchange it for a pair of frilly knickers.'

And so the bantering and bartering began. My face was sore laughing, especially when he moved in on Keriann.

She clutched her glass of champagne and judging by the whites of her eyes, I don't think she expected him to grab the glass and her, and down the champagne in one as he held her upside down. He boogied the full length of the living room. Keriann squealed with delight as he twirled her above his head. She missed the fringes of the lampshade by a hair's breath.

Mrs Sherry snapped the whole thing with her phone. She had it set for scandal.

'I want Brodan to see how Keriann enjoyed herself,' Mrs Sherry said to me.

'Kiss my swingers,' MacNeil shouted after putting Keriann down safely and stripping off to his sporran in time to the music. The women clapped and encouraged his scandalous behaviour. I may have joined in. Shame on me, ahem. I hoped Fergus had kept his binoculars in his drawers because MacNeil certainly wasn't wearing any.

Everyone gasped. His sporran was big but not quite large enough to hide his personables.

'Give us your sporran, MacNeil,' one of the women shouted. I think it may have been Mrs Sherry but I wasn't entirely sure. There was so much shouting, cheering and raucous laughter. And a lot of that was coming from MacNeil.

Ceard pretended to cover Eila's eyes as MacNeil mounted an armchair and used the lace doily in ways that I couldn't have imagined.

'That's my lace doily,' shouted Mrs Sherry. 'Put that down.'

MacNeil threw it aside, complaining that the lace was too rough and snagged the hairs on his legs. And other bits.

His wild dancing continued. He was fit. I'll say that for him. His stomach muscles were toned and his physique honed to strong and lustful levels that most women can only dream of.

A few of them would be dreaming about him tonight. Many of their men were in for a full night's activity.

Lots of the women wanted to feel MacNeil's muscles. He went round the room flexing his bulging biceps and giving them a feel of his rippling manhood. I am of course referring to his biceps.

Mrs Sherry clutched his arm and gave it a squeeze. 'Oooh, you're a big strong one.'

'I could lift you up like a wee feather.' Without giving her a chance to refuse or run, he grabbed her and held her above his head. Careful not to knock the lampshade, he then shouted, 'Okay, Mrs Sherry, up you go.' He proceeded to thrust her up to full stretch and balanced her with one arm. Then he dipped her at speed, causing her to scream, and pumped her up and down like a bar–bell.

When he put her down she staggered and so he lifted her up and insisted on giving her the kiss of life. She later whispered to me that it was probably the kiss of her life.

'It's the first time I've ever felt so hot wearing my cotton pinny,' she confided, fanning her face with a napkin in the kitchen.

MacNeil came bounding in, making the tiny kitchen feel like a giant had arrived in a doll's house.

'Any ginger left?' he asked her.

'Plenty for you,' she said, flirting with him. She poured a large glass of lemonade for him. 'Do you want a scoop of ice cream in it?'

'Aye, sling it in,' he said, smiling down at her. Despite all the women who'd made mild or blatant offers to entertain him later that night, he seemed genuinely fascinated with Mrs Sherry. No offence, but I wondered what he saw in her. She certainly didn't flaunt herself.

He leaned down and I watched his strong–boned face focus on me. He wasn't my type, but rarely had I experienced such a close–up of raw masculinity that had no shame in declaring his desires.

'I'm trying to persuade Mrs Sherry to go out with me. And you should encourage her to wear shorter dresses.'

She tried to shut him up but he continued to reveal a secret.

'She's got long, showgirl legs,' he said. 'She should show them off. Wearing just her pinny and high heels earlier she confirmed that she's as gorgeous as I thought she'd be.'

He bounded off again.

Mrs Sherry put the jug of lemonade back in the fridge.

'Your pinny and high heels, eh?' I nudged her and she started to giggle.

'Don't tell anyone,' she insisted. 'He caught me at a weak moment. It had been a busy day and I'd lots to organise for this evening. It was his idea that I lie down on the sofa and put my legs up for a wee while.'

I laughed so loud that Ceard heard me and made a beeline for us.

'And well...one thing led to another.' She smiled and fussed with her hair.

'That was a dirty laugh,' said Ceard. 'You two are up to something.'

Mrs Sherry looked guilty.

Ceard nodded. 'So one of you has been up to something with MacNeil,' he surmised.

'It wasn't me,' I said. Then I noticed Fergus walking past the cottage trying to have a look in.

He walked on. I sighed with relief. This wasn't a party that would suit him. Was it? I couldn't picture the bespoke tailor shaking his tail feathers and propositioning women who wore a flowery pinny. Fergus wasn't the type. Was he?

Chapter Nine

The Tea Dance

As Ceard gave a demonstration of how to create a French plait, I saw Fergus walk past the window again. It was obvious he was trying to nosey at what we were up to. What *I* was up to.

I slipped out without anyone really noticing and called after him. He came over.

'I was just passing,' he said.

Yeah, right. I smiled at him.

'Okay so maybe I was curious,' he admitted. 'How is the party going?'

'It's lively. MacNeil twirled Keriann around the living room. And I think she enjoyed it. He did one–arm lifts with Mrs Sherry and thinks she should wear her pinny more often. And only her pinny with high heels. I've had lemonade and ice cream.'

'You sound as though you're the only one behaving well.'

'Definitely. The others have been shocking, especially when MacNeil was stripped down to his sporran.'

'I could never compete with that.'

'Oh, I don't know,' I teased him. 'With the right music, I'm sure you could give MacNeil a run for his money. You could wear one of those fitting waistcoats, an extra long tie and a pair of brogues. I'd include braces but I shudder to think what you'd have to attach them to.'

Fergus considered the ensemble. 'Waistcoat, long tie and brogues. What would I wear with that?'

I smiled at him.

'Oh, I see.' He cleared his throat. 'I doubt I'd ever wear that unless I'd lost a stupid bet.'

I was in a playful mood. 'Want to make a stupid bet?' I wasn't being serious but somehow we'd started to wind each other up. The warm night breeze wafted through the fabric of my summery dress but our conversation was hotting up.

'Okay, what will we bet on?'

I said the first thing that sprang to mind. Later I wished I hadn't but it was out of my mouth before I could reconsider. 'Let's bet on

Brodan and his tea shop. I think that Keriann will encourage him to cut the lease short and leave before the end of the summer.'

'I don't think so. Brodan is strong–minded when it comes to business. He'll want to make the most from the lease. I think he may even extend it and keep the tea shop open until Christmas, providing the pop–up agreement allows for this.'

'It does. I know the pop–up girl personally so I can confirm this is absolutely true.'

He smiled at me. 'If you lose the bet, what do you have to wear? Something suitably embarrassing.'

'A flowery pinny and high heels.'

'Is that it? An apron and heels?' I could hear his mind whirl picturing that outfit.

I nodded and we shook hands on it.

'Did I just make a stupid bet with you?' he said.

'Uh–huh. And regardless of what Brodan does with his tea shop, one of us will have to dance for the other in the centre of your lounge with suitably upbeat music.'

'Can you dance, Jayne?'

'Don't sound so confident, Fergus. It's going to be a long, hot summer. You might want to get some practise in dancing in those brogues.'

We gazed at each other for a moment and once again, he looked more handsome than ever. Perhaps it was the light sparkling off the sea, or maybe I just liked him a little bit more?

I heard the women cheer from inside Mrs Sherry's cottage.

'I'd better get back to the party.'

'Enjoy the rest of your evening.'

'I will. I may even indulge in some more ice cream.'

'Living on the edge, eh?'

I nodded. 'Oh yes. Vanilla and strawberry here I come.'

He walked away to his house and I rejoined the party.

'What did Fergus want?' Ceard asked me.

'We were discussing him dancing half–naked wearing a pair of brogues.'

'Remind me never to get involved in any of your bets, Jayne.'

'I've got a pair of brogues,' MacNeil chipped–in. 'When I tap dance in them everything shoogles.' He went to give us a demonstration.

Ceard held up his hands. 'We can picture it, thanks.'

'Awe, don't be a spoilsport,' one of the women said to Ceard. 'Let MacNeil shoogle if he wants to.'

Without needing any encouragement, MacNeil, now almost suitably dressed, wearing his kilt, sporran but no shirt, gave the girls a demo of his shoogle action.

And so the party continued into the twilight hours.

The majority of women were still partying as I headed home. Mrs Sherry thanked me for helping her keep on top of the dishes. I told her I'd pop into the tea shop to see her soon.

As I was leaving, trouble was continuing to brew.

'Oh, look what MacNeil's done with one of my lovely tea towels,' Mrs Sherry shouted.

He was wearing it as a thong.

'I can never dry my crockery with that again without thinking where it's been,' she said.

'It was lucky you didn't see what he did with your tea strainer,' said one of the women. 'Bleugh. Dirty rascal.'

Mrs Sherry scolded him. 'Keep your danglers away from kitchen utensils, MacNeil, or I'll show you what I can sieve through a colander.'

He thrust his hips out at her and did the closest to exotic dancing that a man of his size could manage.

The women screamed. I wasn't sure if it was entirely complimentary.

By the time I got back to my flat I was up to my eyeballs in ice cream, lemonade, a glass of champagne and sore laughing. A great night was had by all, including Keriann. I'd like to say that she was okay once you got to know her but that would be a whopper of a lie. She was actually snippier than even I had anticipated but no one took any snash from her, especially Mrs Sherry who had photographic evidence of Keriann cracking a smile and being hurled around the living room by MacNeil.

The next morning Donel phoned me at home. He was so wound up he didn't give me a chance to even say hello

'Don't say that I told you, but Mrs Sherry is gossip fodder.'

'Why is that?'

'Someone...' he coughed. 'Keriann...reported her for scandalous behaviour in a public place. The police were called and there's a rumour that she was caught canoodling with MacNeil half–naked in the pansies. Oh shite, here she comes. I have to go.'

I couldn't stand the suspense so I went to the tea shop on the pretence of wanting a cream tea that morning.

Donel seated me at a table and brought my tea, scone, jam and cream over. 'Mrs Sherry's through the back putting ice cubes in her rollers. She's got one hell of a hangover. See if you can wangle the details out of her before Keriann and Brodan arrive.'

'Could you attend to the customers while I roll out my scone dough?' Donel said to her. 'I want to see if there's any way I can increase my length by another inch or so with the porcelain rolling pin.'

Wearing a very neat chiffon scarf to cover her rollers, which didn't look out of place in the vintage tea shop, especially as her apron matched, Mrs Sherry attended to the tables. She looked knackered but brightened up when she saw me.

'What happened?' I whispered to her.

'After you left last night I started drinking the hard stuff,' she said. 'After three glasses of sweet sherry I was blootered. MacNeil was leaving and flirting with me, threatening to haul me into the flower beds and have his wicked way with me, but I beat him to it. I grabbed him and someone phoned the police and reported us. Luckily, by the time the police arrived MacNeil had scarpered and I pretended I was in the garden plucking mint for my cooking.'

'Did the police believe you?'

'Nah, but they came in for tea and cake and there's nothing more to come of it.'

'Well, that's okay then.'

She nodded and then remembered the hangover and steadied herself. 'I've got a thumping headache. Two sherries is my limit. Never again. Never.'

'I've got more ice cubes for your rollers,' Donel said to her from the kitchen.

'Thanks, Donel.' And off she went to get them.

Brodan drove up. Keriann wasn't with him. I sat at a table by the window and sipped my tea and ate my scone as if nothing was wrong.

He nodded at me and went straight through to the kitchen.

I listened and heard Brodan tell them that Keriann had left and that he needed to go up to Glasgow to talk to her.

'Is it because of the photographs?' said Donel.

'What photographs?' Brodan asked.

I heard the silence. Brodan obviously didn't know about the photographs that Mrs Sherry had taken of Keriann and MacNeil.

'No photos,' said Mrs Sherry.

'What photographs, Mrs Sherry?' Brodan insisted.

I remembered she'd told Keriann that if she didn't stop being cheeky to her she'd send a couple of the photos to Brodan. Keriann didn't give a hoot and dared her to send them. She even gave her Brodan's number so she could send the photos to him. Mrs Sherry had pressed the buttons on her phone in a determined manner and pinged the pictures to him.

There was a pause. I assumed Brodan was checking his phone.

After he calmed down he stormed out of the tea shop saying he was driving up to Glasgow and would be back later.

Donel and Mrs Sherry came over to me.

'He wasn't happy when he saw the photos of Keriann,' said Donel.

'He seemed upset already,' I said.

'I think madam and him had an argument again last night and she took off up to Glasgow. He's running after her. Love, eh? More trouble than it's worth sometimes. I'd rather have a cup of cocoa and a film on the television.'

'And a rumble in the roses with a big kiltie,' Donel added.

Several customers paused and we moved the conversation into the kitchen.

Donel had managed to increase the size of his dough and pressed out the scones with a cutter while more scandal was revealed.

I watched his technique. 'I've always wanted to improve the height of my scones.'

'Never roll the scones too thin. Have them at least three and a half centimetres. Press the cutter down on the scone mix to cut it out. Don't twist it or the edges of your scones could be ragged or wonky. I never shoogle my cutter when it comes to scones.'

'Have you any wee tarts left?' a customer called through to us.

'No, she's gone back up to Glasgow,' Mrs Sherry muttered.

I smiled.

Donel went to attend to them. 'Rhubarb or plum?' he said.

'What's going to happen now to the tea shop?' said Mrs Sherry.

I shrugged and thought about my bet with Fergus. The odds were in my favour. He'd need to start practising with his brogues on.

'You've got a faraway look to you, Jayne,' she commented. 'Are you okay?'

'Yes, I was going to mention to Brodan about having a tea dance as a promotion for the tea shop.'

Mrs Sherry seemed to forget about her hangover. 'An old–fashioned thé dansant?'

'A what?'

'A tea dance. I used to go to them years ago in one of the old halls before it closed. They sometimes called them tango teas. Waltz and tango were the popular dances. We'd have afternoon tea and dance. I loved them.'

'Fergus suggested we have one in his house. His lounge has a floor that's large enough. We thought that cakes from Brodan's tea shop could be used to promote the business.'

'We could still go ahead with it.' She sounded so enthusiastic. 'Brodan will be back once he's sorted out Keriann. And if the dance is organised by Fergus and you it can go ahead anyway.'

'Fergus wants it.'

'That's settled then. I've got photographs from back in the day. I'll bring them in and let you see what the hall looked like. Sometimes we had a live band, but other times we just played old songs.'

'I've got a vintage tea dress that I could wear.'

'I'm sure I've got a couple of my old dresses lurking in the back of my wardrobe. I had a pink satin dress. Every time I wore it I felt great. I never threw it away. It'll be in my wardrobe somewhere. I'm actually a wee bit thinner than I was back then. Life has worn me to the bone, Jayne. But a summer tea dance, now that would be wonderful. All the girls who were at the party last night would definitely go and we could advertise it in the tea shop window.'

That was the start of our plan. During the next few days it kept us going, planning the tea dance and pushing aside all thoughts that Brodan could abandon the tea shop and wipe away our hard work and efforts to make things nice. When it came right down to it, we cared more about the tea shop than him. So we made our plans and Fergus moved the furniture from his lounge and hired tables and chairs for the guests to sit around the edges of the dance floor.

We scheduled the dance for the second week in June. The weather was supposed to be warm and Fergus wanted to have the patio doors open so that people could wander out on to the lawn and dance outside while enjoying the sea air. It sounded perfect. Brodan kept in touch with Fergus from Glasgow. He was still trying to placate Keriann who had heard that he'd been flirting with me and with Eila. Keriann was the jealous type and even the smallest spark of suspicion could set her off. Even though her behaviour was less than prim, she set her own standards and hated when Brodan was even mildly interested in anyone else.

While they continued their drama up in Glasgow, we worked at the tea shop. Donel took on the role of manager. Mrs Sherry was in charge of nearly everything else including baking her shortbread and specialities. Donel had his own baking talents, as did Eila, and together they created such a wonderful range of cakes, scones and fresh bread for the tea shop. Fergus dealt with the finance, the banking and checked on Brodan's parents' house. So even without him, we were managing fine, and the tea shop was increasing in popularity. Other party nights were booked, and Ceard helped out when he could. And the tea dance was going ahead with or without Brodan McBride.

Behind the scenes Fergus had a surprise for Mrs Sherry. Not really for her personally, but something he thought she'd like. I was sworn to secrecy.

The weather during the first week of June was warm and by the first weekend it was so hot that I had to sleep at night with the windows open. I kept hoping that it would remain like this for the tea dance. Wafting around in a chiffon tea dress on the lawn of Fergus' house sipping cocktails or having tea wouldn't be the same if it was raining.

On the day of the tea dance Ceard's salon was jumping. Numerous women in the town wanted their hair done specially for the occasion and Ceard had even hired extra staff to deal with the demand for vintage hairstyles.

I arrived at Fergus's house a couple of hours early. The tea dance was starting at 4:00 p.m. and continuing into the twilight hours. We had enough tea, cakes and sandwiches to feed the town. Or at least to keep most of the guests happy. Other bakers in the town were involved, and it became one of those events where everyone chipped in. A cocktail bar had been set up.

All the tickets sold like hot cakes, or should that be tea cakes? Fergus extended the capacity by hiring a marquee to cope with the overspill and more tickets were sold. The event was advertised in the local paper and part of the proceeds were being given to a local community centre to fund further afternoon tea dances.

Dress shops in the town benefited from increased trade, and Isa's sewing shop was inundated with customers wanting tea dresses made from her vintage–style fabrics. If I hadn't already owned a dress I'd have had her make me one from the fairy cake fabric. I planned to wait until she was less busy and ask her to make me a dress anyway.

Although Fergus had been busy with his tailoring business, and a few more men had decided to buy suits from him, there was one customer who received special attention. This man couldn't have afforded a bespoke suit. Thousands of pounds for a suit were sort of out of his price range, so Fergus made it for him free of charge. He also gave a classic, gentleman's dinner shirt and tie to Donel who was delighted to be given these. Ceard had even managed to cut and restyle Donel's hair to get rid of the cockatoo tufts.

A local band, dressed in dinner jackets, were hired to play classic songs in a corner of the huge lounge and Fergus had back–up music when they needed a break.

Fergus welcomed me in. He wore a classic white dinner jacket and black trousers. Very art deco era I thought, but his slicked back hair and handsome features carried it off. My heart ached when I saw him. We'd become closer recently and although we'd yet to spend our first intimate night together, I knew that we would. At least, I hoped we would. Ceard was still dating Eila, and although in another life he would've been the man for me, in this one it was Fergus.

'You look beautiful, Jayne.' Fergus kissed me lightly, careful not to mess up my vintage red lipstick. My floral dress felt cool in the hot summer afternoon. The dress fitted fine and didn't need any alterations.

'All set?' I said, feeling the excitement mount.

'As ready as we'll ever be.'

Fergus was being modest. He was well–organised. Brodan was still in the city and had been vague about his plans. Sometimes he said he'd be back for the tea dance, and other times he said he couldn't make it. I think his world depended on Keriann and his business in Glasgow had genuinely needed him to be there. He shouldn't have taken on the tea shop. There was no space in his life for it. It saddened me to think that the tea shop would close soon. Brodan had hinted to Fergus that he was due to shut up shop even though it had made a profit. No thanks to him. Thanks to Donel, Mrs Sherry and Eila, and Ceard and Fergus. And yes, me. We'd all kept it ticking over because it deserved to be there. Customers would miss it too. But nothing lasts for ever, I kept telling myself.

I pushed all thoughts of the tea shop from my mind and looked forward to the tea dance. People were starting to arrive. They were all dressed up, and as they got out of their cars and then walked along the promenade to the house in the bright sunshine, they looked as if they were part of a painting from the past with the brilliant blue–green sea in the background.

Some of the ladies wore hats and fascinators. All the men wore suits and a couple of them had hats too.

I felt quite teary for a moment seeing the bother they'd gone to. Everyone looked top–notch. From that first night when I'd thrown the idea into the conversation with Fergus to seeing what we'd created, filled me with pride and happiness.

The band began playing and at 4:00 p.m. the tea dance was declared officially open.

Couples took to the dance floor.

'Would you care to dance with me?' said Fergus.

I smiled and nodded.

He led me on to the dance floor and we waltzed as the sea breeze blew gently into the lounge.

'Whatever happens this summer,' I said to him as he held me in his arms, 'I'll remember this day.'

'Me too,' he said. We waltzed around the room with people we knew, some nodding acquaintances and others we'd never met before. Everyone blended into the atmosphere of the tea dance as the band played classic romantic songs.

Chapter Ten

Cakes, Scones & Romance

Sunlight glinted off the sea. The house was slightly higher than the level of the promenade and each time we danced past the wide open doors and looked out at the seashore I felt as if we could dance right out on to the surface of the sea.

The early evening brought more warmth with it, along with more people, dressed in their finery.

Mrs Sherry looked lovely in a blue dress that was a fair match for the sky, though now hints of pink and lilac were creating a subtle fade to the landscape. The islands in the distance were hidden behind a pale blue mist unless you shaded your eyes from the sunshine striking off the water and noticed their beautiful outlines on the West Coast horizon.

Donel switched roles continuously. Sometimes he was a guest and danced with the ladies. Sometimes he helped at the lavish buffet, making sure the silver cake stands were topped up with everything from classic Victoria sponges and Battenberg to the fabulous ice cream cakes that were in a refrigerated display and looked so perfect some people thought they weren't real and for display only. The delight on their faces when they realised they could have a slice of such perfection was worth every scalloped edge and smooth as ice finish on them. The depth of the layers of vanilla, strawberry and chocolate ice cream was sheer luxury.

For those who wanted to feel that they were enjoying themselves at the seaside, harking back to happy childhood days when the summers stretched out for weeks on end, old–fashioned ice cream cones which were listed as pokey–hats were available. I planned to indulge in one of those, so when Fergus swept us around the dance floor one last time before we took a breather, I asked if I could have a cone to cool me down.

'What flavour would you like?' said Fergus.

Lots of flavours had been added to the classic vanilla, including chocolate fudge, caramel, mint and champagne. Donel and Mrs Sherry had requested an ice cream machine and had experimented with various flavours including tea.

I opted for smooth vanilla with raspberry sauce. Fergus had a strawberry cone and we wandered outside to enjoy them. The sky arched above us and the golden glow from the amber sun gave Fergus's white dinner jacket a sepia tint. He looked even more as if he belonged to a traditional era than ever.

I finished eating my cone and glanced back at the house. 'I'm determined to live in a house by the seaside. I'm going to work hard so that I can afford to rent one of the cottages. A cottage like the one Mrs Sherry has.'

'Would it have to be a cottage?'

'No, why?' I wondered if he'd heard about a vacant property.

He pointed up to the top floor of his house. 'See that skylight window right at the top?'

'Yes.'

'You can see the entire bay from there. I used to sleep in one of the master bedrooms at the back, but then I moved into the skylight room. It's a bit smaller but I can lie in bed on a clear night and gaze up at the stars. When it was snowing in January it felt like I was living in a wonderland. And on rainy nights there's nowhere cosier in the world.'

'It sounds amazing.'

'It is. And so are you, Jayne.'

He was gazing at me now.

He took my hands in his. 'You must know that I'm in love with you. And I'd like to hope you like me too.'

My heart melted. Like him? I more than liked Fergus. 'I feel the same about you.'

'I was thinking of inviting you to stay the night with me. I've been thinking this for days now. Then I thought...no, I've always loved to do things the traditional way and when it comes to something as special as this, I thought I'd take a chance and do this properly. The old–fashioned way. Sort of.'

I wasn't sure what he meant but the butterflies in my stomach were threatening to take off with me as the excitement built up.

'I thought that if we started dating I'd end up asking you to marry me and presenting you with a ring.' He paused and looked slightly nervous as he pulled the silk handkerchief from the top pocket of his jacket and inside was an aquamarine and diamond ring set in white gold. The aquamarine was as blue as the sea at the height of summer and the diamonds sparkled like the light glinting off the sea.

He was asking me to marry him? I felt my world tilt. I knew that Fergus loved me. I did. I'd sensed it for a while now, and I knew it was only a matter of time before we became a couple in the truest sense. But this...this...? A proposal?

'I thought I'd ask you to marry me, Jayne. And that when we became close and spent time together it would be as a couple. A couple who were promised to each other. A couple with a future, not just a summer romance that would fade when the autumn arrived. I wanted you to know that I've never, ever, felt this way about anyone. Not anyone. Except you.'

I was smiling at him and nodding. 'Yes, Fergus. I'd love to marry you.'

He slipped the ring on my finger and it sparkled in the light and I knew I'd made the right choice. Fergus was definitely the one for me.

He leaned down, pulled me close and kissed me, and a cheer erupted from inside the house. People had been watching us.

I blushed and we gave them a wave.

Then Fergus' expression became concerned.

'Is something wrong?' I said.

'There's something I have to tell you and I'd rather do it now than later. Brodan phoned just before you arrived. His parents are coming home. I won't need to tend to their house. They'll be back in a couple of days. They missed being home and decided to return early.'

'Well that's okay, isn't it?'

'Yes, but there's something else. Brodan's also asked me to close the tea shop for him. He's not coming back. He's staying in Glasgow and dealing with his business there. He wants me to pay off the staff, give them a bonus for everything they've done, and also to give a bonus to you. The pop–up girl.'

He'd called me the pop–up girl?

'That's what annoyed me. Sometimes I'd like to shake some sense into him. We've always wanted different things. I've always wanted to settle down and get married. Brodan is never content with anything. He's successful at what he does. He's a master pastry chef but he creates chaos and leaves other people to clean up his mistakes.'

'Are you going to close the tea shop for him or let him come down and do his own work?'

'I've told him I'll deal with the tea shop. I don't want him to come back down. I'd prefer him to stay in the city for quite a while actually.'

A sadness swept over me. The tea shop days were almost over.

'I don't want to let the tea shop go just because Brodan doesn't want it,' said Fergus.

My heart jolted. 'Really? What do you plan to do?'

'Well, the lease is paid until the end of the summer. Brodan has no intention of reneging on the pop–up deal which is something to his credit. So I was thinking that as I'm not a baker and neither are you we've got a bit of a problem if I were to take on the lease of the tea shop. We'd need staff to run it. A reliable manager who'd open up and be able to bake cakes, scones and was an expert at etiquette.'

'It might be difficult to find one of those,' I said, smiling.

'And a woman who works well with him and bakes great shortbread.'

'A tea shop needs shortbread.'

We laughed and I leaned up and kissed him. 'You'll keep Donel, Mrs Sherry and Eila?'

'Of course. And we'll meddle in things obviously, but I think it will work. Don't you?'

'Yes, it will work. The tea shop is popular and now that Brodan isn't in the mix we'll be able to run things the way we want. Brodan was hardly ever there. He baked a few cakes but it was Donel and Mrs Sherry who did the work. It was their baking and ice cream that people enjoyed. The shop was already kitted out as a tearoom with the tables and everything. All Brodan added was the curtains upstairs and it was Isa who made them for him. The crockery, teapots and cake stands are his obviously.'

'I'm having everything that belongs to him packed and sent up to Glasgow. Brodan knows I'm taking on the shop now and wishes me all the luck.'

I could feel the excitement building up inside me. Suddenly the tea shop felt free to flourish even more.

'You'd have to arrange an extension on the pop–up lease,' said Fergus.

I smiled at him. 'No problem. After all, I'm the pop–up girl.'

We burst out laughing and any resentment we'd felt towards Brodan melted in the mellow sunlight.

We went inside and told the others our plans. There were champagne and tea toasts all round. And cake and ice cream.

Mrs Sherry gave Fergus a hug. 'Oh I'm so pleased you're taking over.'

'Me too,' said Donal.

'I'm happier to work at the tea shop when it's just us. I never felt at ease with Brodan or Keriann,' said Eila.

Ceard proposed a toast. 'To new beginnings.'

We all drank to that.

Mrs Sherry looked around. 'I thought that MacNeil would be here by now. I know he was working late but I'd promised him a dance.'

Fergus saw MacNeil walking up the esplanade. 'Here is he now.'

Mrs Sherry frowned. 'Where?'

And then she realised that the tall, well–dressed man, walking along proudly wearing his new bespoke suit was her handsome kiltie. The classic three–piece dark suit was worn with a white shirt and silk tie.

'Is that MacNeil?' she gasped. 'Oh my, he looks handsome in that suit. Where did he get a suit like that? It looks like...'

We were smiling at her.

'Fergus made it for him,' I told her. 'He thought that a fine figure of a man like MacNeil would look great in a suit. It's a gift.'

Mrs Sherry smiled at Fergus. 'That was very kind of you, Fergus. You're a lovely man. You've made my man look like a proper gentleman.'

'Your man, eh?' Donel gave her a wink.

'He's been asking me to date him,' said Mrs Sherry. 'And seeing him in that suit, I think I'll keep him.'

The tea dance party continued into the late evening. As the sun sizzled down into the sea, people left the party in a happy mood.

Cars drove off, and various couples opted to walk home along the promenade on the lovely warm evening.

Mrs Sherry was seen walking arm–in–arm with big MacNeil. Fergus had certainly affected a few hearts that night.

We waved the last people away, and for the first time I felt like the lady of the house, standing with my man, with Fergus. The sea breeze continued to waft across the coast and I gazed up at him for a moment. He smiled and enveloped me in a passionate kiss in front of the house.

I breathed in deeply and cleared my throat. 'You're a very good kisser,' I said, smiling.

'It's a handy thing you only have to put up with it forever then eh?'

We both laughed.

'Why don't we take a walk on the beach and watch the sunset,' he said.

The suggestion was perfect. 'That sounds wonderful.'

Fergus grabbed a set of keys and closed the doors. We wandered down to the promenade and walked along in the fading sunlight. It had been a wonderful day and I hoped we would host more parties. That's the moment I realised how easy it was to be a couple with Fergus, how easily I could think of being with him and doing everything together. A couple. I liked the sound of that.

'This has been my most perfect day ever, Fergus.'

'Mine too. It's not everyday you get to propose.'

I closed my eyes for a moment and breathed in the fresh sea air.

'I'm so glad I found you, Jayne. Right now life feels complete.'

'I feel the same.' I reached up, put my arms around his neck and kissed him.

And then I remembered something...

'There is one thing that has to be done,' I said to him.

He frowned. 'What?'

I tried not to smile with glee. 'Our bet. I do believe I won. Brodan cut the tea shop from his life before the end of the summer.'

'You don't really expect me to...'

I nodded. 'Oh, yes. Better polish those brogues, Fergus, and practise some dance moves.'

He laughed.

'A bet is a bet,' I said. 'A fitted waistcoat, extra long tie and a pair of brogues. I'll let you off wearing the braces.'

He lifted me up and held me in his strong arms. 'You really want me to dance half–naked?'

'That was the bet and I aim to collect — with bells on. Or in your case brogues and a tie.'

'You might just get more than you bargained for, young lady, making demands like that.'

'Oh I do hope so, Fergus. I really do.'

We never told anyone, but after our walk along the promenade, we went back to the house and Fergus went through to his sewing study while I set my chair up in the lounge to enjoy the showpiece. The music was set to play at the press of a button. My finger was poised. We kept the lights dimmed to prevent anyone being shocked seeing the bespoke tailor letting himself go wild. It was a private, one–night only performance, though after seeing the moves he made, I insisted we include this in our romantic repertoire. Something to be brought out when we needed to liven things up.

'Music maestro,' Fergus called through to me from the hallway before strutting into the lounge wearing...well...the sexiest bespoke outfit I'd ever seen. I wanted to pop those buttons on his waistcoat as he did his first twirl around the dance floor. Fergus could move. And what a gorgeous lean, strong torso he had. The fitted waistcoat emphasised his fit–looking, muscled chest and broad shoulders.

'I was right. You can certainly give MacNeil a run for his money,' I shouted to him as he shimmied past, flicking his tie at me. Okay, so he'd kept his underpants on. But not for long. I clapped and encouraged Fergus to go all the way. We were engaged now after all and so very traditional.

He pulled me on to the floor and we danced together. Those brogues of his were made for dancing the night away. I could barely keep up with him. We danced all the way upstairs to his bedroom.

During the summer the tea shop flourished and so did our various romances.

I continued with my pop–up work, finding premises for new businesses. I loved my work. And I loved Fergus.

Fergus was right about the view from his bedroom. When we snuggled up in bed at night we could gaze up at the stars and listen to the sounds of the sea as we drifted off to sleep.

We could peek out and see the lights from the tea shop shining in the near distance. Fergus had added vintage lamps outside the shop and a string of little fairy lights along the frontage.

Sometimes the traditional things in life are worth more than anything. The tea shop with its cakes, ice cream and afternoon tea was worth everything we all put into it.

I stood at the window gazing out at the town and at the tea shop. Our tea shop.

Fergus wrapped his arms around me and kissed me, soft kisses on my neck that sent tingles through me.

'Come to bed, Jayne,' he said. 'The tea shop will be there in the morning.'

I smiled up at him and then glanced out the window before snuggling up in bed with Fergus.

The lights from the tea shop sparkled in the distance.

Even when it was closed for the night the lights on the outside still glowed in the dark, promising that the tea shop was merely pausing for the evening to catch its breath and would open up again each morning to serve traditional cakes, scones and delicious ice cream.

End

About the Author:

Follow De-ann on Instagram @deann.black

De-ann Black is a bestselling author, scriptwriter and former newspaper journalist. She has over 80 books published. Romance, crime thrillers, espionage novels, action adventure. And children's books (non-fiction rocket science books and children's fiction). She became an Amazon All-Star author in 2014 and 2015.

She previously worked as a full-time newspaper journalist for several years. She had her own weekly columns in the press. This included being a motoring correspondent where she got to test drive cars every week for the press for three years.

Before being asked to work for the press, De-ann worked in magazine editorial writing everything from fashion features to social news. She was the marketing editor of a glossy magazine. She is also a professional artist and illustrator. Fabric design, dressmaking, sewing, knitting and fashion are part of her work.

Additionally, De-ann has always been interested in fitness, and was a fitness and bodybuilding champion, 100 metre runner and mountaineer. As a former N.A.B.B.A. Miss Scotland, she had a weekly fitness show on the radio that ran for over three years.

De-ann trained in Shukokai karate, boxing, kickboxing, Dayan Qigong and Jiu Jitsu. She is currently based in Scotland.
Her colouring books and embroidery design books are available in paperback. These include Floral Nature Embroidery Designs and Scottish Garden Embroidery Designs.

Also by De-ann Black (Romance, Action/Thrillers & Children's books). See her Amazon Author page or website for further details about her books, screenplays, illustrations, art and fabric designs.
www.De-annBlack.com

Romance books:

Sewing, Crafts & Quilting series:
1. The Sewing Bee
2. The Sewing Shop

Quilting Bee & Tea Shop series:
1. The Quilting Bee
2. The Tea Shop by the Sea

Heather Park: Regency Romance

Snow Bells Haven series:
1. Snow Bells Christmas
2. Snow Bells Wedding

Summer Sewing Bee
Christmas Cake Chateau

Cottages, Cakes & Crafts series:
1. The Flower Hunter's Cottage
2. The Sewing Bee by the Sea
3. The Beemaster's Cottage
4. The Chocolatier's Cottage
5. The Bookshop by the Seaside

Sewing, Knitting & Baking series:
1. The Tea Shop
2. The Sewing Bee & Afternoon Tea
3. The Christmas Knitting Bee
4. Champagne Chic Lemonade Money
5. The Vintage Sewing & Knitting Bee

The Tea Shop & Tearoom series:
1. The Christmas Tea Shop & Bakery
2. The Christmas Chocolatier
3. The Chocolate Cake Shop in New York at Christmas
4. The Bakery by the Seaside
5. Shed in the City

Tea Dress Shop series:
1. The Tea Dress Shop At Christmas
2. The Fairytale Tea Dress Shop In Edinburgh
3. The Vintage Tea Dress Shop In Summer

Christmas Romance series:
1. Christmas Romance in Paris.
2. Christmas Romance in Scotland.

Romance, Humour, Mischief series:
1. Oops! I'm the Paparazzi
2. Oops! I'm A Hollywood Agent
3. Oops! I'm A Secret Agent
4. Oops! I'm Up To Mischief

The Bitch-Proof Suit series:
1. The Bitch-Proof Suit
2. The Bitch-Proof Romance
3. The Bitch-Proof Bride

The Cure For Love
Dublin Girl
Why Are All The Good Guys Total Monsters?
I'm Holding Out For A Vampire Boyfriend

Action/Thriller books:
Love Him Forever
Someone Worse
Electric Shadows
The Strife Of Riley
Shadows Of Murder
Cast a Dark Shadow

Children's books:
Faeriefied
Secondhand Spooks
Poison-Wynd
Wormhole Wynd
Science Fashion
School For Aliens

Colouring books:
Flower Nature
Summer Garden
Spring Garden
Autumn Garden
Sea Dream
Festive Christmas
Christmas Garden
Christmas Theme
Flower Bee
Wild Garden
Faerie Garden Spring
Flower Hunter
Stargazer Space
Bee Garden
Scottish Garden Seasons

Embroidery Design books:
Floral Nature Embroidery Designs
Scottish Garden Embroidery Designs

Printed in Great Britain
by Amazon